John King

Sprays, leaflets and blossoms

John King

Sprays, leaflets and blossoms

ISBN/EAN: 9783337281892

Printed in Europe, USA, Canada, Australia, Japan

Cover: Foto ©Andreas Hilbeck / pixelio.de

More available books at **www.hansebooks.com**

Sprays,

Leaflets and Blossoms.

BY JOHN KING.

Not mellow fruit nor branches we,
But sprays and leaflets from that tree —
The evergreen of poesy

London:

JOHN WILLIAMSON, 93, DRURY LANE, W.C.

SCARBOROUGH: J. C. HODGSON, SAINT NICHOLAS CLIFF;

GEO. KYTE - GRICE, SAINT THOMAS STREET.

MDCCCLXIX.

TO

THE RIGHT HONOURABLE THE

EARL OF DERBY, K.G.

THIS VOLUME

IS HUMBLY AND MOST RESPECTFULLY

DEDICATED.

Preface.

As I have been solicited by numerous friends to prepare a volume of my poems and verses for the Public, I have collected this edition, bearing the title of " SPRAYS, LEAFLETS, AND BLOSSOMS," which are dedicated, by kind permission, to the Right Hon. the Earl of Derby. It will be acknowledged by every thoughtful mind that it is better to strive to elevate our position in society, socially, morally, and intellectually, than to degrade ourselves by a lifetime spent in vice and misery. If so, my readers will not consider me presumptuous in introducing this little work, coming (as it does) from the very heart of the working-classes. Not from that class that enjoys the fresh air and lives in the sunshine, and is enchanted by the music of birds and brooklets, and whose home lay by the flowery paths of the woodland,—no, but from the heart of the pale-faced artisan, who breathes the contaminating and poisonous atmosphere of the narrow and overcrowded workshop ; from that class that is shut out (as it were) from the world, and from all that is pleasant and beautiful. Of this class the author of the present work is a member, and my readers are aware that it is difficult to " sing the Lord's song in a strange land," therefore they will not expect me to please the refined scholar, my aim being to spread morality and refinement of taste amongst the class to whom I belong, and to see it rise from ignorance and oppression to intelligence and freedom, is the sincere desire of the reader's

Humble Servant,

THE AUTHOR

Scarborough, June 22nd, 1869.

Contents.

Amy de Clare — — — — — — 1	The Cuckoo — — — — — — 56
Allan of Alnwick — — — — 15	Come roam with me — — — — 56
Alice de Courcey — — — — 25	The Red Flag Waves — — — 57
Lily-crowned May — — — 33	The Dying Girl's Vision — — 58
Edith of Lea — — — — — 34	A Boy to a Robin — — — — 59
To my Lyre — — — — — — 37	O, I would be a Butterfly — — 60
A Glimpse of the Mount — — 38	The Zephyr-Kissed Gem — — 60
To the Morning — — — — 40	Summer — — — — — — 61
Twilight — — — — — — 41	An Autumn Song — — — — 62
What is the Echo — — — 42	Dreamland — — — — — — 63
The Blossoming Bilberry Tree — 43	Arise in the Morning — — — 63
An Invitation — — — — 44	The Snow Flake — — — — 64
The Temperance Star — — — 45	Summer Comes — — — — 65
The Streamlet — — — — 45	The Emigrant's Farewell — — 65
The East may Boast — — — 46	The Speedwell — — — — 66
Sonnet — — — — — — 46	The Hare Bell of the Down — — 67
Impromptu — — — — — 47	The Fields their Emerald Robes put on 68
My Cot shall be the Home of the Free 47	Violets — — — — — — 68
Spring — — — — — — 48	Autumn — — — — — — 69
The Laugh of the Children for me — 48	I have Watched by Moonlight — 70
Evening — — — — — — 49	Musical Trent — — — — 71
To Scarborough — — — — 50	Beauty will not last for aye — 72
Amalgamation — — — — — 51	The Woodland Maid — — — 72
Our Joys are Brief — — — 52	To May — — — — — — 74
To Miss E. P—— — — — — 52	Jennie's Snowdrop — — — 75
The Star of Freedom — — — 53	The Talking Ox — — — — 75
Wilson's Wood Valley — — — 54	To Victory or Death — — — 77
Stanzas on a Primrose — — 54	This World is not the Wilderness — 77
The False and the True — — 55	To the Reader — — — — — 79
Dropping Leaflets — — — 55	

Sprays, Leaflets, and Blossoms.

AMY DE CLARE.

A TALE OF SCARBOROUGH AND THE NEIGHBOURHOOD.

WHERE on the gray rocks by the deep
The snowy crested billows leap,
And evermore the mighty sea
Is uttering its melody,
And where the sea-gull wings its flight
Over Scarboro's rocky height,
There dwelt a knight of great repute,
With heart more callous than the brute.
A shrill blast from a bugle blown,
His castle doors are open thrown,
And cometh from the castle yard,
Knight Percy with his body-guard.
On they sweep with the falcon's speed,
Each mail-clad hero and his steed,
And soon beneath the sun's broad light,
Each glittering form is lost to sight.

There stands a castle, run's the tale,
That guards the entrance to a vale,
Known as the Forge, and there once dwelt
A knight who oft for others felt.
This was the gallant Lord De Clare,
With Amy his sweet daughter fair,
And oft beside the Derwent stream,
Beneath the bright and golden beam
Of lovely Sol, did Amy stray,
And plucked the lilies on her way,
Or in the hall at Ayton, she
Would hail the knights of chivalry.

B

'Twas in the joyous month of May,
When Amy from her tower gray,
Was watching for her sire and love,
Lord Howard, from the lands above.
The gay laburnum's golden boss
Was falling on the grass and moss,
And in its frail and emerald boat
The water-lily was afloat;
The voice of spring alone is heard,
The gentle carol of the bird,
The willows where the breezes sweep
Had sung the sentinels to sleep.
And now they have arrived there,
Lord John of Howard and De Clare.
The order goes from Amy fair,
" The servants must a feast prepare,
And to partake I shall invite
Castle Howard's noble knight."
They sat them down in the great hall,
And here and there upon the wall
Were hung rare trophies of the field,
The banner, lance and brazen shield.
But hark ! there thunders through the glen,
Like the sweeping of a hurricane,
An armed host, and at their head,
Knight Percy, with his plume blood red.
The knights exchange a transient glance,
Feel for their swords, in haste advance.
With tumult doth the castle ring—
What saith that voice?—" News from the king !
Peace, knight De Clare, the task is ours
To go against the northern powers !
To Howard's Lord we now must hie,
Such news should like the lightning fly."

" Brave Percy, now at Ayton stay,
Since Howard's Lord is here to-day,
He will himself the news convey,
And get his men in full array."
Thus spoke Lord Clare, and Howard's knight
Did greet bold Percy with delight,
And said, " the news I now must bear
I cannot longer linger here,
But take my leave with every grace—
Let noble Percy name the place
Before I beat this rude retreat."
Percy replied, " Then be it so.
Our men must at Saint Hilda's meet,
And we the chiefs at Scarboro'.
The men must meet at early morn,
Before the lark hath left the corn.

The chieftains, ere the silver moon,
Shall lift its orb the hills aboon—
Brave Howard and his dauntless throng
Will startle half the Scotch ere long."
But ere the last words from him fell,
The knight was sweeping through the dell,
And proudly in the noon-day light
Shone that plume of spotless white.
Through Ayton's hall the cry hath gone—
"Go meet the Caledonian!"
But Scarhro's chieftain for awhile
Was revelling in Amy's smile:
"In Ayton's stream no lily fair
Can equal thee, sweet child of Clare!
Say wilt thou, maid, accept the hand
I offer thee as here I stand?"
"I cannot," was the prompt reply—
"Then, maiden! may I ask you why
You now refuse a knight so free?
Doth Lady Clare object to me?"
"Farewell, sir knight, I must depart,
I thank you from my inmost heart,
I am betrothed unto the knight
That rode away with plume so white."
"Then as I've now made free to task
You, linger, maiden, while I ask
If now the noble Lord de Clare
Of your bethrothal is aware."
"The daughters of the house of Clare
Clandestinely would never dare
Offend their sire at such a time—
He had got his consent ere mine.
Adieu! brave knight! I now must go—
I wish you victory o'er the foe."
The callous knight, then, swore that he
Would take revenge on all the three;
And ere it tolled the hour of one,
Knight Percy and his men were gone.

    Now o'er the mountain and the moor,
Where the ocean loud doth roar,
Thousands of mail-clad heroes push,
Trampling on the ling and rush,
And over bush and over broom,
And o'er the furzes golden bloom.
Above the bay of Robin Hood
Howard's dauntless men are stood!
See! them—waving in the air
The sable plumes of gallant Clare!
And Percy's braves—a noble line!
See how their lofty red plumes shine!

Knight Percy comes—arriving there,
He asks for Howard and great Clare.
Said Howard's captain, " by your leave,
He left us early yester-eve,
On milk-white steed, said, he must go,
O'er hill and dale to Scarboro'."
Then Clare's bold captain, pale with fright,
Said, " Clare left Ayton's hall last night,
With Howard's chieftain by his side,
For Scarboro' the knights did ride :
We took the Forge, and met your men
Below the hill at Burnisten."

   " What stranger knight, so young and fair,
Is that now with the men of Clare ? "
" A nephew of brave Clare's, they say,
That came to Ayton yesterday."
" Then why not at Saint Hilda's meet ?
Must I my orders now repeat ? "
" What makes us pitch on Robin's brow ? *
The Scotch are at Saint Hilda's now.
They are arrayed in noble line—
See, how their polished sabres shine !
Now listen to the bagpipe's song,
Inspiring all that Godlike throng,
And now their banners are unfurl'd,
Threat'ning death to half the world,
And o'er their heads their feathers wave,
Like freedom's banners o'er the brave !
And now the hardy bare-limbed race,
Are moving at a steady pace."
But quick as thought doth Percy's eye
   Along the line of mail-clads glance,
The sword that swingeth by his thigh
   Is, flashing, drawn, he shouts, " Advance ! "
The sable plumes of noble Clare
Are tossing in the centre there,
And Howard's on the left will be,
The red ones waving next the sea,
Quick march ! the cry, and they are gone,
And martial music cheers them on ;
Ten thousand horsemen now I see,
And fifty thousand infantry !
And now the dogs † of vengeance bark,
And make the golden moorland dark.
What mean the foe ? their lines so long
Are marched against the white-plumed throng ;
Their famous chief with brazen shield,
Now thunders, " Haughty tyrant ! yield ! "

   * The moor above Robin Hood's Bay.
    † The booming cannon.

But Percy's voice with mighty sound,
Shouts, " Men of Howard ! stand your ground !
Charge, knight De Clare ! and on you go,
Ye red-plumed throng from Scarboro' ! "
And now the hissing snakes * of war,
Are spitting venom from afar,
The clash of arms is spreading wide,
And groans are heard on every side,
The Scotch are driven to the rill,
The white plumes are triumphant still !
Now see the knight so slim and fair,
That leads the men of gallant Clare !
His sword is like the falcon's wing,
Quick flashing like fork'd-light'ning's spring !
The Scotch now press with all their might
Against the red plumes on the right,
On ! on they go with dauntless will,
And drive the red plumes down the hill ;
They chase the English to the sea,
Their chieftain shouts, " to victory ! "
See Percy's braves prepare for flight,
    And terror seizes every rank,
But Howard's horsemen swift as light,
    Are striking on the foemen's flank.
Knight Percy's ranks are broken now,
    The breach is healed by Howard's men,
Dealing death at every blow,
    The hardy Scots recoil again.
Now the slim knight, young and fair,
Is leading on the men of Clare,
He waves his sword, and on they push,
And trample on the ling and rush,
Striking home, and every blow
Lays some hardy Scotsman low,
On comes the mighty foeman chief,
    And slays the captain of bold Clare,
He rushes to his men's relief,
    And presseth on the knight so fair ;
With vengeance flashing from his eye,
    He strews the ground with heaps of slain,
The slim knight's sword doth swiftly fly,
    The chieftain's skull is split in twain.
The victor now doth pause for breath,
The Scottish toads † are spitting death,
On that day, 'neath the gallant fell
Six horses in that bloody dell.
See ! Percy's foot re-charge again,
His horsemen thunder through the glen ;
Before the mail-clads and their steel,
The valiant sons of Scotland reel,

    * The musketry.   † The cannon.

They quail, they tremble—do they fly?
Ah! no, they conquer or they die!
See how the bare-limbed race withstand
The iron-armoured English band!
Fierce the conflict now is raging,
Hand to hand they are engaging,
From the swords the blood is streaming,
As they beneath the sun are gleaming,
Loudly is the war-horse neighing,
Over-head the raven straying,
Hark! the groaning of the dying!
Are their lovers for them sighing?
The shades of night are now increasing,
And the noisy tumult ceasing.
Sweet night hath come to chase the day
From the bloody field away.
" Hail! tranquil night, so calm and fair,
To those stretched on the stain'd sod there;
They heed thee not, bright evening star,
Twinkling in the heaven afar!
But O, the groans, the sobs, the sighs,
That from the battle-field arise,
They tell me with a voice so plain,
That man is callous, weak, and vain;
When on the wings of passion borne,
He is its slave, he is its scorn,
His heart how hard, and in his will
How little good, how much of ill!
The heart of man is the retreat,
Where angel, and where devil meet."
Thus spoke the valiant knight so fair,
While tending on the dying there.
And Percy sat within his tent,
When Howard's captain to him went
To ask about the missing knights.
" How gallantly that youngster fights?"
Burst from the lips of Percy brave,
" Exultingly his sword did wave,
Six times the valley he hath cross'd,
Six noble chargers he hath lost,
He slew the mighty Scottish chief,
And ordered us to your relief;
He is the hero of the glen,
    Skull after skull his sword hath cleft,
For out of thirty thousand men
    They have but half that number left.
Our loss, as I now ascertain,
Is over twenty thousand slain:
Your Lordship's foot are swept away,
And only ten have left the fray;

Three hundred horsemen are the most
That Scarboro's gallant knight can boast."
Percy replied—" The loss is great,
For reinforcements I must wait,
And you and Clare must take your men
And chase the Scotsmen back again;
But of the knights I nothing know—
They also may have been laid low."

Next morning from the slumbering sea
The men arose triumphantly,
And sweetly shone o'er hill and dale,
And over Robin's peaceful vale;
And on the brow of Robin stood,
Weeping o'er the scene of blood,
That field of havoc and of gloom,
The lovely knight of sable plume!
The Scotch had softly crept away
Soon after darkness closed the fray,
And nowhere could the foe be found,
In glen nor in the moor around.
Knight Percy shouts—" Press on! I'll take
My men, and follow in their wake!"
They march, he lingers looks behind,
Some mocking voice upon the wind,
Seem'd plainly to the knight to tell,
'Twas there the crest of Percy fell.
They reached Saint Hilda's on the moor,
The foe had left the night before;
Beneath the sun's bright scorching rays,
They had a fruitless march for days;
But when the hills arose in view,
Knight Percy from the chase withdrew.

'Tis rosy June, and Ayton's bowers
Are scented by the summer flowers;
But where that lily of the lake?
Doth she the Derwent stream forsake?
For missing sire the lady grieves,
Beneath the trembling aspen leaves.
But oh! where is the gallant Lord,
Whom Amy's trusting heart adored?
The hills are searched and every dell,
But no one of the chiefs can tell,
And Amy's heart is troubled so,
In haste she starts for Scarboro'—
'Tis gained, and at the castle gates
The maiden for admittance waits,
The massive doors move on their track,
Like two old surly giants back,
Astonished that a maid so fair,
Should enter that grim portal there.

She reached the hall, the feudal chief,
Addressed her thus,—" You seem in grief?
What happy chance hath brought you here,
Madam?" as a satanic sneer
Lurked about his firm-set lips—
" 'Tis sorrow's cup my lady sips."
" And can knight Percy thus address
The child of Clare, in her distress?
And she upon bereavement's brink?
It soundeth strange, and makes me think
That you, my Lord, possess the key
That can unlock the mystery."
" The daughter of the house of Clare
Is now as bold as she is fair,
To thus accuse a gallant knight
In his strong castle on the height,
Where he can hail the peep of morn,
And look down on the world with scorn
And watch the sun far in the west—
My castle is the eagle's nest,
And I the bird, my talons keen
Have in the flesh of Howard been,
And now the lark of Clare shall sing
Until the eagle's nest shall ring:
The maiden shall her father see."
He calls, " a torch—the dungeon key!"
And bids the maiden follow him
Through the gloomy fortress grim.
The torch then cast a lurid light
On sullen walls and fearful knight.
And on the lovely maiden presses
Through the castle's dark recesses;
Now with the knight she is alone,
Passing down the steps of stone,
And they have reached the dungeon door,
It, groaning, opens, on the floor,
Stretched upon the damp stones there,
Lay Howard's knight and gallant Clare.
And Amy, standing in the porch,
Saw by the glimmer of the torch
Her gentle sire and lover bound
With iron fetters on the ground!
She sprang into the dismal cell,
Exclaiming, " Howard," shrieked and fell.
The damp, cold floor was then her bed,
Her reason and her senses fled.
Life's tint returneth to her face,
Her heart is throbbing to embrace
Her friends; she riseth, and each knight
Is kissed in anguish and delight;

Then to knight Percy she doth fly,
And fix on him her dauntless eye,
Saying, with true dignity of mind—
"Why are those gallant knights confined."
And Percy, looking on the while,
Beheld their sorrow with a smile,
For in his heart, so black and dire,
Revenge was burning like a fire.
" I made an offer once," said he,
And the fair maid rejected me,
And she preferred the gallant knight
That rode away with plume so white.
And on that day I swore to be
Revenged, young maiden! on the three,
And smiling fate put in my power
The knight of Clare, and rival flower ;
But this sight maiden is the best,
The lark is in the eagle's nest,
And now the lark must sing and sigh,
And say which gallant knight shall die ;
For blood alone can quench the fire
That rages with a keen desire."
And then the daughter of brave Clare,
She wrung her hands and tore her hair,
Then falling at the demon's feet,
Upon her knees she doth entreat ;
But useless were her prayers, and vain,
The choice is hers—one must be slain.
For would the wild-cat spare the dove,
Because it sang of peace and love ?
The hungry tiger quit the fawn,
Because it gamboll'd on the lawn ?
Or would the miser quit his hold,
When he had grasped the precious gold ?
Nor will *he* swerve from his design—
Then, maiden, say, the choice is thine !
And then the sorrow-stricken knight,
Whose raven-hair had turned to white,
Whose cheeks were pale with want and grief,
Said—" Daughter of a gallant chief !
O come and press me to thy heart,
For from this world I would depart—
Yea, I, my child, would sooner be
Dead, than chained in misery.
Then, demon Percy, know that I
Am now prepared, and wish to die ;
But from the house of Clare will spring
A lark to clip thy eagle wing."
" The choice was not for thee, knight Clare !
But granted to thy daughter fair.

Haste guards!" he cried, and down they pour
To see kneel on the dungeon floor
The Lady Clare,—" O how can I,
Bid thee, gentle father! die?
With grief my bleeding heart is torn—
O cruel fate, why was I born?
Must I this dreadful sentence give?
Long, valiant Howard, may'st thou live
To be———"
                    She waved her lily hand
And fell, and then, with stern command,
Did Percy in his hellish ire
Bid his guards behead her sire.
The dungeon rings with piercing cry,
The glittering axe is raised on high!
It falls,—and rolleth on the floor
The trunkless head besmeared with gore.
The fiend then bid his guards convey
Knight Howard and his bride away;
And Amy, senseless and forlorn,
By ruffian hands was rudely borne
With Howard to the castle gates,
And there a convoy for them waits.
"Convey them home!" was his command—
They start with glittering escort grand;
On they sweep, and the castle grim
Fades from view in the twilight dim.
But why should those two lovers ride
Through lovely Hackness side by side?
Cheered by the music of its rills
They reach the vale and sister hills,
And in that narrow mountain gorge,
Known as the lovely vale of Forge,
They meet some fifty mail-clad men,
While Howard's convoy is but ten.
A voice proclaimeth—" halt!" they stand
Like men death-smitten on the land.
Howard, enfeebled and alone,
Demanded in a faltering tone—
"Who bids me halt?"—
                    " A knight, the best
That e'er dwelt in yon eagle's nest,
Percy of Scarboro', it is I—
Howard prepare—you now must die!"
Fair Amy hitherto did seem
Like one enwrapp'd in peaceful dream;
But Howard's name with magic power
Went to her heart, as to the flower
That droops, the fertilizing shower,
Awakening every slumbering power!

She then approached the callous knight,
With eyes like shining orbs of light,
And said, with voice of hate and scorn—
" Is Scarbro's knight of woman born,
Or hell's begotten fiend ? now give
The word—shall Howard die or live ? "
" What doth the Lady Clare suppose
That I shall spare my rival rose ?
The sweetest draught is in the cup
Of vengeance yet, quick, pour it up !
Guards to your work, now bind him fast,
That long embrace will be the last !
Howard commend your soul on high—
By I count twenty you must die."
The maiden's strength at last was spent,
Her shriek of woe the night air rent ;
But ere the sound was from them borne,
The loud blast of a hunting-horn
Startled the mail-clads, and they found
Their men were falling to the ground :
Arrows showering thick and fast,
Like hailstones on the sweeping blast !
The poisoned and the swift-winged darts
Were biting at the mail-clads hearts,
And Percy quickly raised his eye—
" On every side I do descry
A lawless band of green-coat curs—
The heights are thronged with foresters !
Fly ! fly ! to horse ! quick ! follow men ! "
He spurs his war-horse through the glen,
And now a fierce and feathered dart
Hath pierced his charger to the heart—
And down the valiant green-coats rush,
Springing from each bower and bush ;
Another charger he hath gained,
The steed is mounted, spurr'd and rein'd,
And on he sweeps with eagle flight,
The arrows follow swift as light,
From every side they do assail,
And rattle on his suit of mail—
The chargers, rushing to and fro,
Are riderless, and on they go—
The outlaws raise a cheering cry,
They mount each steed away they hie,
And madly they the chase persue
And soon each form is lost to view !
But ere the knight could reach the plain
Full forty of his men were slain.
Amy, awakened by the cry,
Observed the rushing horsemen fly,

And, glancing round, unhurt she found
Her fallen lover helpless bound,
And quickly did the maiden go
To yonder grim and prostrate foe,
His sword, then hanging him beneath,
Was swiftly flashing from its sheath :
"And this, brave knight, is done for thee—
Thy bands are cut and thou art free!
She bids him follow with a smile—
"To Ayton Hall, 'tis scarce a mile!
Quick, Howard, should the knight return,
With fiery rage his heart will burn."
But Ayton's halls are reached at last,
The danger and the fear hath past,
And soon a band of valiant men
Were clattering through the peaceful glen.
From Ayton are the heroes sent,
To Castle Howard they are bent—
But, hark! what saith the maiden fair ?—
"Come, listen, men of gallant Clare!
'Tis not the northern foe alarms,
Your chieftain's blood calls you to arms,
'Twas shed by Scarboro's callous knight,
In his grim dungeon on the height."
Death and vengeance was the cry—
A thousand swords were raised on high,
A host of heroes then were rife
To fill the eagle's nest with strife.

        Hark! the shrill bugle now proclaims
The morning o'er the earth's domains,
And calls each mail-clad to his post,
And o'er the vast and valiant host
Their chieftain's death hath spread a gloom ;
But Howard wears a sable plume,
And when that gallant knight they see,
They shout —" he leads to victory!"
Now list! the soul-inspiring drum,
And see the men of Howard come!
Ten thousand plumes of spotless white
Are waving in the morning light ;
The mingled hosts do loudly hail
The slim knight in the shining mail :
"'Tis he!" they shout—" so young and fair,
That led the men of noble Clare!
See his impatient charger prance,
And now he bids the troops, advance!"
The sounding music and the fife,
That nerves the hero for the strife,
The accents of the trumpet shrill,
That to the wav'ring gives the will,

The stately and the measured tread,
That fills the feeble mind with dread,
The din of arms, and all the shine,
Attending on each martial line—
All this the young knight saw with pride,
As on he marched at Howard's side.
They now behold the mighty deep,
As on they push down Stepney's steep,
And Percy from his tower sees
Their bannerets that kiss the breeze—
" To arms," he cries, " let every man
Throng each fort and barbican ! "
The white plumes now at Wallsgriff stay,
The men of Clare march to the fray,
And o'er the head of Howard brave,
That sable plume doth proudly wave.
Death and vengeance now they cry—
Their crimson banners flaunt on high,
They see that Percy's force is small,
And go against the southern wall.
Knight Percy from within now sees
Them eager swarm, like stingless bees ;
But on they press with all their might,
And plant their ladders on the height,
And thunder at the sullen walls,
Till many a gallant hero falls ;
And now a breach has been obtained,
The lofty battlements are gained,
And Clare's proud standard is unfurled ;
   But quickly there doth Percy run,
With rage the standard down is hurled,
   Now has the deadly strife begun,
And Howard's heart doth burn with scorn ;
   He caught the colour ere it fell,
And proudly is the standard borne,
   To be placed on the citadel.
The rolling of a thousand drums
Proclaims another army comes ;
They grandly move, led by the knight,
With shining mail and plume so white.
The men are marched the gates before,
The rams are thund'ring at the door,
It bends, and into splinters flies,
And at his post each vassal dies.
The drawbridge gained, the ditch is past,
The inner door is reached at last,
And quickly from its hinges hurled,
And swiftly down the gray rocks whirled.
Before the young knight's fiery eye,
See how the men of Percy fly !

Now past their chief the white plumes push,
And at the foe with vengeance rush.
The men of Clare do hotly press,
They are inflamed and merciless ;—
Hark ! to their cry, as on they go—
" Revenge, and death to every foe !"
See, yonder ! Percy fights for life,
With but ten comrades in the strife.
His eyes are like fierce flames of fire,
His heart now burns with hellish ire,
And how the gallant white plumes reel,
And fall beneath his reeking steel.
But now there rusheth to the fray
A knight that fills him with dismay ;
His sword doth flash as swift and free,
As lightning plays upon the sea !
Confronting Percy, with a bound,
He struck him helpless to the ground ;
And Percy saw before he fell,
Knight Howard on the citadel ;
The standard planted was the best
That e'er waved o'er the eagle's nest,
The flag of Clare was proudly borne,
And Percy's trampled on with scorn,
And over Scarboro's fallen chief,
The slim knight shed a tear of grief,
And cast his helmet from his head,
That Percy might, ere he was dead,
In that young gallant knight so fair,
Behold the orphan Lady Clare.

———

ALLAN OF ALNWICK.

THE BOWMAN OF NORTHUMBERLAND.

A TALE.

COME, tender muse, and aid me now,
With rose and myrtle on thy brow!
Erato, of the glorious nine!
Fill with fire this heart of mine!
Apollo! on my rude harp be,
And strike the strings of harmony,
With music let thy temple ring,
While I of faithful lovers sing!
Diana, spotless goddess, now
Seated on great Olympus' brow,
Ascend thy car, preside thee long
O'er the subjects of my song.
For Bonnie Annie was as chaste
As any flower on moorland waste;
And Allan was a hunter free,
And loved to roam as doth the bee.
O may my invocation rise,
And reach thee in the fabled skies!
Olympus leave, and with me stray
To where the Tyne rolls on for aye!
See! now she comes, the goddess bold,
With chariot of shining gold,
And white stag chargers passing by—
Behold her! with the poet's eye!

Where the Tyne's waters 'neath the sun,
Through mead and woodland winding run,
And, gilded with his cheering rays,
Are purling their sweet roundelays,

Like Naiads on each gentle swell
Playing on their lyres so well,
That every soul must feel the charm
That lingers here at twilight calm.
Here stands Prudhoe, so famed in story,
With towers gray and turrets hoary,
Arising 'neath the bright blue sky,
Yet not more bright than Annie's eye,
As she within the garden straying,
Was with bud and blossom playing,
And the flowers she loved so well
She plucked for Lady Isabel.
A flower more fair ne'er sprung from earth
Than Annie though of lowly birth ;
She was the Lady's waiting maid,
In love and modesty arrayed—
A form more graceful never sate
Enthroned nor wore a coronet.
Her heart was pure, her mind was chaste,
From danger she would flee in haste.
And when a yeoman pressed his suit
Her cheek would blush, while she was mute ;
Then, raising her dark eyes, would she
Decline his suit with courtesy,
And in reply would softly say,
" Her lover dwelt not far away.
But in the glen was often seen
Young Allan in his Lincoln green,
And often had his fatal dart
Quivered in the fleet deer's heart."
And when he heard young Allan's name
The yeoman pressed no more his claim,
But in a bumper bowl would quaff
To him and Annie Bickerstaff!

" Hark! what music softly falls,
And echoes round the castle walls?
'Tis Pan that plays upon his flute.
And yet it murmurs like a lute.
Hush! now again methinks I hear
The voice of Annie sounding clear ;
Again that plaintive strain repeat—
Ye Gods! it sounds most wond'rous sweet!
'Tis Annie with my mother sings
Her vespers while the castle rings.
Choice game, I trow, the girl is fair—
What splendid eyes and lovely hair!
By all the saints and Virgin Mary,
I'll keep an eye on that young fairy,
And if she foils Odênel, then
My bones may bleach in yonder glen!

Thus spoke the Lord of Prudhoe's halls
As he was pacing 'neath its walls.

The sun arose, the eastern skies
Were blushing with vermillion dyes,
And on that calm September morn
The dewdrops sparkled on the thorn;
The air was humid, and the breeze
Sighed gently through the forest-trees;
The bursting bud, the blushing flower,
Were wet with dew that early hour,
And with the lark did Annie rise
To see bright Phœbus gild the skies,
To sit within the sylvan nook,
And listen to the merry brook—
To pluck earth's fragrant gems, and say
Or sing her morning roundelay.
And there, with folded arms, was seen
Hidden amongst the foliage green—
There, like a statue, and as still,
He stood—Odênel Humfraville.
The maiden knew not he was there,
So she enjoyed the morning air,
And the swift brooklet loud and long
Symphonied to her early song.
She saw the corn upon the scythe
Falling before the reapers blithe,
And bound together into sheaves,
While round her fell the faded leaves.
A noise within the thicket near
Then made fair Annie start with fear,
She fled into the garden ground,
And was afraid, for there she found
The knight Odênel Humfraville.
" Good morn, fair Annie, roaming still ?
Astir among the flowers, I ween—
What sayest thou, come, and be my queen;
Once press thy rosy lips to mine
This costly bracelet shall be thine."
" Base knight, though I am lowly born,
I spurn you with a woman's scorn !
Not while the flowers spring from the dust
Will I be servile to your lust,
I would that noble Allan knew
This hateful insult, you would rue ;
One shaft sent from his good yew bow
Would lay you, lustful tyrant, low."
She turned and quickly fled away,
Like a fawn before the hounds that bay,
Nor did she stay till, safe and sound,
She in the castle hall was found.

D

Odênel, pacing to and fro,
Was wrath he let the maiden go.
" The saucy jade my will to chide,
Nor scrupled she to wound my pride.
This very day, upon my soul,
I'll have her under my control.
I would, said she, that Allan knew—
This forester she loves as true
As dove its mate—what's he to me ?
I vow, ye gods, revenged I'll be !
I'll splinter lance, make good steel ring
With this outlawed forest king ;
His arrows may be swift and sure,
My armour they will hurt no more
Than snowflakes hurt the granite wall,
As they so softly on it fall !
But who comes here me to annoy ?
A wee fair-headed peasant boy.
What brings you here, my boy, I say,
So early on an autumn day,
To steal our apples do you roam ?
If so, you'd better hasten home."
" I came not here to steal, sir knight,
For stealing is not my delight ;
I came to see the tinted flowers
In famous Prudhoe's fragrant bowers ;
In wood, cool grove, and glen I've been—
The flower I seek I have not seen.
From Eltringham the maiden came.
And Bonnie Annie is her name ;
To see the maid I now require,
I bring a message from her sire."
" You know the maiden then, my boy ? "
Replied the knight with inward joy,
To find already in his power
The fairest gem in Prudhoe's bower.
" Ah, no, I know her not, but then
Such bonnie looks we always ken."
" Then to yon shady bower retreat,
And rest you on the rustic seat,
And, as you have not had your lunch,
These rosy apples you may munch,
And from that bower you must not stray
Till Bonnie Annie comes this way,
And if our grooms should seek to fright
You, start not, boy." " No sir, all right ! "

How cool the grove, how fair and bright
Were the pure beams of golden light
Peeping through green branches, where
Sat the poor boy with flaxen hair,

When came a female tall —said she,
" So this young gallant seeketh me."
The boy her costly vestments eyed,
And was abashed as he replied—
" Your pardon, ma'am, I wish," said he,
"The Bonnie Annie here to see."
" Then am not I a bonnie one
With all this costly raiment on ? "
" No, by the waters in the brooks,
Rich garments give not bonnie looks ;
But if you be fair Annie, then
I bring a token you should ken."
" A token, boy-- we have two or three,
The brooch and locket bought for me.
Our token now, as I 'was told,
Should be the ring of shining gold."
" Here is the ring, now lady tell
The motto—you should know it well,
Then you shall have the ring and hear
Some news from one who loves you dear."
But here the lady was at sea ;
She did not know it—why should he ?
But from suspense she soon was freed,
She found the poor boy could not read.
Saying unto him, " farewell—adieu ?
The motto must be fast and true."
" Ah ! that is it," the lad replied,
And told his message, then he spied
Ripe apples on a neighbouring tree,
To those she helped him merrily,
And as the boy went on his way,
He, speaking to himself, did say—
" If thou art bonnie, by my hair !
I've seen a maiden thrice as fair."

From a lone room in Prudhoe's tower
There watched a modest spotless flower,
That flower was the maiden fair,
With love-lit eyes and wavy hair.
Ye Gods ! what love, what joy and bliss,
Were centred in a form like this,
Did ever mortal 'neath the skies,
Gaze on such beseeching eyes ?
So full of love and holy trust,
Her soul how tender, pure, and just !
He, blessed with such a faithful soul,
Is blessed indeed as planets roll ;
Her love shall light him to life's close—
O chasten'd joy ! what sweet repose !
With such a one, so free from vice,
'Twould turn a hell to paradise !

And from that tower there watched a maid
Who in those virtues was arrayed ;
She was alone, her heart was sad
To see the young and bashful lad
Met by the knight, poor lustful cur !
Who knew the message was for her.
She heard him speak a word or so,
Then saw him to the cook-wench go :
The lewd girl came, gay dressed, to play
Fair Annie's part, and won the day,
And when she had dismissed the boy,
She met the knight, who laughed with joy,
And when she had the message told
He gave the wench a coin of gold.
And Annie like a woman bore
Her troubles, though they vexed her sore.
Sweet Zephyrus had gently blown,
And rook and dove to roost had flown ;
The sun the western hills had gained,
And Muta o'er the woodland reigned :
'Twas eve, that sweet and tranquil hour,
When Annie left old Prudhoe's tower,
And wandered lonely through the vale,
Where plowers told their twilight tale.
She nothing in the woodland feared,
And was by sweet Concordia cheered.
And hastened on, all thoughtful still
About her parents who lay ill.
She saw the swains return from toil,
And heard them speak of flock and soil,
And many a smile the old men gave
To her so beautiful and brave.
Her soul with nature was in tune,
Here with her God she could commune.
Pomona, with her mellow store,
Was pleasing as she was of yore :
And when she passed the orchards by,
She saw the tear in Flora's eye.
O say, which was the sweetest there,
In nature's trio of the fair ?
The fragrant flower in woodland shade,
The rosy fruit, or blushing maid ?
Were I a Paris, as I live,
The apple to the maid I'd give !

　　Twilight was fast approaching, when
The maiden reached the hazel glen.
And to the sage the glen is sweet,
A shelter from the summer heat.
And sweet it is to see the flowers,
That deck a glen in springtide hours.

Poets, the gifted race of song !
Would linger here the summer long,
And bending o'er each little flower,
Discern great beauty in the bower ;
In fragile leaf, and verdant sod,
Would trace the wisdom of a God.
A glen is sweet to lovers too,
They seek its shade at eve to woo.
A glen is peaceful in its kind,
And suited to the lover's mind ;
There undisturbed he dreams of bliss,
Forgetting life's realities.
And to the man that lives by prey,
And shuns the open light of day,
A glen is dear, for there he waits
In ambush, while his wicked mates
Lay dosing in a fitful nap,
Reclining on dame nature's lap.
But Annie seemed to know no fear,
To her that glen was ever dear,
And at the close of that fine day,
She sped along the bridle way.
The hare and rabbit crossed her path ;
And reached the middle glen she hath,
And in the gloom 'twas sweet to see
The dear and ancient trysting tree ;
But Annie's heart grew sad with care,
The Bowman Allan was not there.
And from her eye a teardrop fled
For him who might be with the dead.
She sighed and wept, but said she knew
That Allan's noble heart was true.
Fair Annie turned, scarce moved had she
Ten paces from the trysting tree,
When she saw through the twilight gray
Two horsemen in the bridle way.
" Virgin protect me from their plan !
'Tis the knight Odénel, and his man,
Each on a black and prancing steed—
A bridle-horse doth Robin lead."
" Good even ! Annie, whither stray,
My pretty little woodland fay ?
Thou comest to meet thy lover then,
'Neath trysting tree in hazel glen."
" It ill becomes a knight arrayed
To stop an unprotected maid ;
The parents who have loved me so,
Are lying ill, pray let me go,
And stay me not, for they may be
Now passing to eternity."

" Fear not, sweet maid, nor longer roam,
This palfrey shall convey thee home,
And save thy kirtle from the thorns,
Ere glowworm's lamp the glen adorns—
Robin, assist this lady fair
Into the empty saddle there."
Robin dismounted to obey,
But from the serf she fled away :—
" Off, villain, off, or dearly shall
You rue—you hateful menial !
Shame, coward knight! were Allan here
Your base-born hearts would quake with fear."
" I'd dare the devil for one kiss,
And that to-night to me 'tis bliss :
Quick, Robin, quick, this Allan may
Yet mar our sport in this affray.
He seized the maid without remorse,
And bore her to the saddle horse ;
The woodman from his pleasant dreams
Was wakened by the maiden's screams ;
The glen was ringing everywhere,
And cries for Allan rent the air ;
The rook that roosted overhead
Affrighted took to wing and fled ;
The owlet shrieked, the timid hare
Did flee into the covert there,
The foxes bark, the watch-dogs bay,
The rabbits frighted fled away.
Odênel took some silken bands,
And bid serf Robin hold her hands ;
He bound them o'er her mouth, said he,
" I'll stop your merry minstrelsy."
And though the maiden's voice was still,
The echoes on the distant hill,
Like fairies or the elves of sound,
Were calling Allan all around.
" On, Robin, on, the twilight fades,
This Allan may be in the shades !
Quick, man, go first, forget all fear,
Th emaiden next, I in the rear
Will keep this outlawed dog at bay,
Should he molest us on our way.
At my hunting lodge beside the stream
To-night shall lovely Annie dream,
There she shall like a goddess dwell,
My last, my lovely harem-belle."
The echoes they had died away,
The watch-dogs they had ceased to bay,
And from the glen there came no sound,
Save noise of hoofs upon the ground.

Twang—went a bowstring, and a dart
Quivered in serf Robin's heart ;
He falls—his master, riding aft,
Then came to extricate the shaft—
" Ah! cursed fate, 'tis now I know
It came from outlawed Allan's bow."
Before he could withdraw the dart,
A shout of triumph made him start ;
A plumèd chief in Lincoln green
Leap'd from a thicket near the scene,
And called—" Surrender! tyrant knight !
Or now prepare thyself to fight."
" Surrender now, I ask to whom?
Ah! just consider, sir, thy doom,
Thy only weapon is a bow,
My sword would quickly lay thee low."
" To Allan, the forest outlaw, he
That cares not for thy tyranny ;
Though at this bow thou dar'st to frown,
It brought thy servile jackal down,
And were I now its string to pull,
This shaft would penetrate thy skull."
" Ah! well, if thou wilt have thy way,
Thy flesh shall feed the birds of prey,
This maid shall hear thy dying groans,
The forest-cat shall pick thy bones!
Now mark my word, my armour, sir,
Is strong, and thou a forester,
Base outlawed-dog, that dares brave me,
I'll ne'er surrender, sir, to thee."
And, with these words, he dealt a blow
That would have laid our hero low,
But Allan, like the nimble roe,
Leap'd away from his angry foe ;
And Allan's faithful boy was near,
He with his master did appear,
And caught the maiden as she fell,
And bore her to the mossy dell.
And he the servile Robin found
Outstretched and vanquished on the ground :
That arrow was the dart of death,
It glazed the eye and stopp'd the breath,
And, quick as thought, the lad untied
The sword from fallen Robin's side,
And reach'd the chief, and then with care
He waited on the lady fair,
With water from a rill that took
Its way unto the distant brook ;
She was refreshed, he did his part
With loving tenderness of heart,

When Robin's sword caught Allan's sight,
He rushed upon the frowning knight,
And called, "Surrender, libertine!
And give to me that sword of thine!"
"No, never, outlaw, while those trees
Can wave unto the evening breeze."
They cross'd their swords, with clash as quick
As lightning, and the sparks flew thick ;
The din of arms was heard till late,
Both skilled in fight and desperate ;
Allan was pressed, but, wheeling round,
He struck Odênel to the ground,
And spilt his heart's blood on the spot
Where Robin was by Allan shot.
And as he fell a shout of joy
Did burst from Allan's faithful boy,
The chieftain's horn in t iumph sung,
Till the vistas of the old glen rung ;
And Annie wept with joy to see
Her lover 'neath the trysing tree.
The hero of her heart had fought—
He had her hand, her freedom bought.
Unto the distant mountains side
Hom ward did the trio ride.
The breeze on Allan's plume did play,
The stars in heaven's milky-way,
A countless host, were shining bright,
The plover shrieked its faint good-night,
The pensive moon, the lovers' friend,
Did light them to their journey's end.
Next morning she at Allan's side
Was made the son of freedom's bride.
Their children now have many cots
Among the breezy Cheviots.
May every lover by them see
That virtue shall rewarded be,
And ever o'er the tyrant's grave
May Allan's plume of freedom wave !

ALICE DE COURCEY.

A TALE OF RIEVAULX ABBEY, YORKSHIRE.

———

ADVERTISEMENT.

THE poem, "Alice de Courcey," is founded on a sad story told ot Sir Walter L'Espec, founder of the once splendid Abbey of Rievaulx, Yorkshire. The Lady Alice de Courcey was the ward of the Lord of Rievaulx, and the destined bride of his son Eustace, the young and gallant crusader.

The splendid ruins of Rievaulx Abbey are situate at the distance of about three miles from Duncombe Park, in a solitary place, near Helmsley, surrounded by steep hills, which are covered with wood and ling, and near the angle of three different vales, each having a rivulet running through it, which, passing by where the Abbey was built, is called the Rye, whence the vale took its name; and this religious house was thence called the Abbey of Rievol, or Rievaulx. The motives that impelled Sir Walter to make over the castle and lands to the Cistercians may be gathered from the following poem.

———

Upon the fruitful lands of Rye
    The castle of great L'Espec stood,
A rivulet flowed smoothly by,
    And murmered through an ancient wood.

The wintry blast swept o'er the hills,
    And to the verdant valleys came,
And froze to ice the puling rills,
    From whence the Abbey took its name.

The sun in splendour shone serene,
    To gild with light Rye's hoary towers ;
And oft within its grounds was seen
    A lovely maiden culling flowers.

Rare charms did that fair maid disclose,
    No peach could boast a sweeter hue,
As fair as any summer rose
    That e'er was bent with pearly dew.

E

And proud was Rievol's aged lord
  Of his loved ward, so young and fair,
And glad to know she was adored
  By his own child, a son and heir.

The maid was rich, her lands were large,
  All this the Lord of Rievol knew,
And when he took his lovely charge
  He had the joint estates in view.

And Eustace loved the Saxon maid,
  And glad was he to find returned
The love for which he so had prayed—
  His heart with tender rapture burned.

Betrothed, he left his destined bride
  Under his father's tender care;
Rievol no fairer form could hide,
  No sweeter flower will blossom there.

And to the East young Eustace brave
  Went a crusader rife for war,
And soon, upon the spray-capt wave,
  He left his home behind him far.

And days rolled on to months and years,
  No Eustace was at Rievol seen;
Though Alice wet her couch with tears,
  Fame decked his brow with laurels green.

The last rays of an autumn sun
  Had tinged with gold Rye's limpid wave;
Its daily course was nearly run,
  Its cheering beams fell on the brave,

When moved a train on slow parade—
  A crusade banner waved in air,
Comes a glittering cavalcade,
  Sir Walter's son, so brave and fair.

In Rievol's hall the lamps were bright,
  The banquet and the merry song—
The dance kept up throughout the night,
  And who could think such moments long?

Alas! sad night, 'twas rumoured that
  Amidst the din and festive glee,
Alone, within her chamber, sat
  The Lady Alice de Courcey.

That night she wore a diadem
  Of priceless wealth, the tale is told,
And sparkled on her breast a gem —
  Her shoes were velvet fringed with gold.

Her eyes were of the deepest blue,
    Her wavy hair was Saxon brown,
Her heart of all things it was true,
    Her face was never made to frown.

In vain she waited for a call
    To bring her to her lover's side,
There came no summons for the ball,
    So she her costly vestments eyed.

" This gem he gave in love, for why ?
    That it might on this bosom shine,
But now my Lord is back at Rye,
    He's left his love in Palestine."

So time can change the fondest heart,
    Though it with truest feelings glow,
Can make it play the traitor's part,
    And find new paths for love to flow.

Rievol's young Lord no more was gay,
    The self-reliant cavalier,
The frank, the fearless flower of May,
    That always had a word to cheer.

Strange fits of sullenness had he,
    And often absent was his mind ;
Fair Alice grieved it secretly,
    And to his will became resigned.

And sorrow seared the lady's heart,
    Her voice was never heard in song,
No lover played the soother's part,
    Nor made the moments flee along.

A coloured servant bore the cup
    Of the young valiant Lord of Rye,
And never would his lordship sup
    But from the hand of Zimbony.

He likewise had a trusted friend,
    That fought beside him on the field ;
Together in the chase they blend,
    And death alone could make them yield.

It fell one day the wine went round,
    The vassals in a merry way,
Then told how their young lord was found
    'Mid ruins of a temple gray.

There with an Eastern princess fair,
    A form so bright, with flashing eyes,
And splendid locks of raven hair—
    A being from the starry skies,

And of a tress so long and dark
   That the master loved to kiss—
They said 'twas brought him by a lark
   From some Eastern court of bliss.

And one day, straying near the hall,
   Lord L'Espec and his friend was seen :—
" My deeds, however, great or small,
   Say have I not a villain been ? "

" Be hushed, my Lord," replied the squire,
   No longer strange and foolish be—
Did not Zelinda you desire
   To wed the Lady de Courcey ? "

" O name her not, my friend, I pray,
   Nor seek to hurt this heart of mine ;
I'll give my hand and lands away,
   And then return to Palestine."

But ere the squire could find reply,
   There started on the humid air
Sweet strains of music, and a sigh
   Breathed from the bosom of some fair.

Soft swell the deep soul-melting strains,
   And falls the tear from Eustace eyes ;
Transported back to distant plains,
   O'er joys departed he did sigh.

And in that music wild and sweet
   He heard the whispering voice of love ;
His fancy saw the cool retreat
   Of nightingale and pensive dove.

He saw a palace beam with light,
   As he stood 'tranced by music's spell,
A lovely form so fair and bright,
   The whispering voice he knew it well.

The youthful minstrel ceased to play,
   Before the castle doth he stand,
A piece of gold rewards his lay,
   From the young Lord of Rievol's hand.

Alice had named the fatal day
   When Eustace should perform his vow ;
Sir Walter give his ward away
   To one so strange and fitful now.

It came, the nuptial day, and went—
   'Twas midnight in the banquet hall,
When Alice to her chamber bent
   From the revelry and ball,

Sir Walter raised his goblet high :
  "To Eustace and his fair young wife,
Ye chieftains drink, ye knights reply—
  A good, a long, and happy life ?"

With blood-red wine each cup was crowned
  At Rievol's stately marriage feast,
Loud did the vaulted roofs resound
  With " Eustace, hero of the East."

O'er Rye's young Lord there came a change,
  Large drops of sweat stood on his brow,
His voice died to a murmur strange,
  His eyes start from their sockets now.

Young Eustace could no longer stand ;
  He was about to leave the place,
When dropped the goblet from his hand,
  And pale with horror was his face ;

For in his wine cup, like a star,
  There shone a graven emerald ring—
How came it there the mirth to mar ?
  What hoary bard its praise could sing ?

The coloured slave that looked so grim
  Was by the squire seen to jeer ;
See ! bound away, a stripling slim,
  Behind the columns disappear !

Alone, within her nuptial bower,
  She sat, the charming Alice fair,
In snowy robes, a spotless flower,
  And round her white neck fell her hair.

On a lily hand her head was bent,
  And gloomy thoughts her mind did greet ;
When one upon the old clock went,
  She raised her eyes—but what to meet ?

A form with sweet surpassing charms,
  There gazing at her she espied,
With jewels on her neck and arms,
  A poignard gleaming at her side.

Before those eyes of dazzling power
  She sunk down motionless and pale—
Why haunt her in her nuptial bower,
  And there her loneliness assail ?

" Ah ! in thee, lady, I behold
  My wedded lordship's Eastern love,
Then speak ! or art thou phantom cold
  Sent here to mock me from above ? "

" Bride of Lord L'Espec " said a voice
    As musical as woodlark's lay—
" Wilt thou forbid me to rejoice
    On this the happy nuptial day

" In her that doth before thee stand
    Behold thy lordship's tender dove ;
To-day thou may'st have ta'en his hand,
    But never can'st possess his love."

Her thoughts confirmed, she strove to speak,
    But all her efforts were in vain,
And glistened on Zelinda's cheek
    A tear-drop she could not restrain.

" Who merits pity more than me ? "
    - Burst from Zelinda's lips in pain—
" But Lady L'Espec ! yet for thee
    Another lord there may remain.

" Though dark and dreadful is the deed,
    I would not have my lady think
Her fair assistance I shall need,
    Should I from its performance shrink."

And, goaded to the utmost verge,
    In vain for help did Alice call,
When awful thunders pealed a dirge,
    And howled the blast o'er Rievol's hall.

" The dead might call from out their graves,
    Your servants could not enter here ;
Thanks to your husband's Arab slaves,
    Who know no law—my frown they fear.

" And since on earth my fate's decreed,
    I'll tell my mission as I stand,
My tale, fair lady, claims a deed
    Of retribution at my hand.

" How, when, or where, I met your lord
    It is not needful here to name,
Suffice to say we met, adored,
    And overwhelming was his flame.

" He ne'er concealed a thing from me,
    Of you he often fondly spake ;
I felt no pang of jealousy—
    I knew love's bands he would not break.

" I had a brother, bold and free,
    Yet of his love I need not tell,
The ripest fruit he plucked for me,
    And fondly called me his gazelle.

" He twined a wreath of flowers fair,
    And gave me, as he said, ' to-day
Unto our camp I must repair,
    Then wear this while I am away.'

" That fatal eve, with Lord L'Espec,
    I sat beneath a pleasant shade,
'Mid ruins of old Baalbec,
    That for wise Solomon was made.

" The moon was up and in high heaven,
    The air was scented with perfume,
That was by fragrant roses given,
    As they the ruins did illume.

" 'Twas love's own hour, alas! alas!
    Our bliss was short—why should I mourn?
That such sweet hours should from us pass,
    And make us to the bitter turn?

" While thus we sat in loving jest
    I heard a footstep passing by,
It was my slave with blood-stained vest,
    Pale face and agitated eye.

" He placed a letter in my hand,
    In which I read, but not in vain—
Read words which made me understand,
    And wrote in fire within my brain."

" 'Thy brother Zelim is no more,
    The last of his illustrious line
Was murder'd by that curs'd Giaour,
    Lord L'Espec, or that love of thine.'

" I gazed on the pale moon above,
    My heart was hurt, my blood was chill,
My brother murdered by my love!
    Then I my duty must fulfil.

" Therefore, I urged him to return,
    That here he might perform his vow;
The fire, revenge, doth in me burn
    To lay my brother's murderer low.

" But hark! I hear his well-known tread!"
    A rap was heard upon the door—
Ere each had time to turn their head
    The bridegroom stood the pair before.

The oaken door he left ajar,
    Nor did his glance fall on the bride,
But on his peerless eastern star—
    He went that instant to her side.

"My own Zelinda! with thy charms!"
　He said with manly passion strong—
She threw herself into his arms,
　And wept upon his bosom long.

When disengaged, she to him said—
　"Fair Lord of Rievaulx, now we meet
To part no more, soon o'er thy head
　The grass and flowers will bloom so sweet."

"Have mercy, maid, thy anger smother,
　Hurt not my heart with coldness now."
"Mercy, murderer of my brother!
　Whose death with laurels decked thy brow

"Why start? 'twas you!" said she in scorn,
　"And here for his revenge am I—
O Allah! that I e'er was born
　To such a cruel destiny!

"We meet," said she, "no more to part,"
　A poisoned dagger gleamed in air,
Then went like lightning to the heart
　Of Rievol's Lord so young and fair.

Proud Rievol's Lord he lay at rest,
　The dagger, crimsoned with his blood,
She took, and fell upon his breast,
　And struck her side whence came life's flood.

And from her lips escaped a moan,
　When the weapon pierced her side,
But Eustace fell without a groan,
　His heart's blood flowing like a tide.

The shrieks of Alice filled the room,
　From banquet hall came great L'Espec,
His son a corpse, sad scene of gloom,
　His ward a raving maniac!

He turned him from that horrid sight,
　A childless, spirit-broken man,
And ever from that awful night
　Fair Alice grew more sad and wan.

Poor soul! thy bard with locks so gray
　Attuned his harp with many a sigh--
He could not sound for thee a lay,
　So sung of the sweet winding Rye.

Still, above Rye's crumbling towers,
　Howls the tempest in its rage,
Blooms a thousand tinted flowers,
　With all their summer equipage.

And shine the stars with steady light,
  The cooling zephyrs blow the same,
The milk-maid sings at morning bright,
  And calls upon her lover's name.

Knight and squire have passed away,
  We hear no more the vesper hymn,
The plantain decks the ruins gray,
  And owlets shriek at twilight dim.

And monk and friar are gone to God,
  And numbered with the silent past,
The halls are empty where they trod,
  And ruined by the bitter blast.

The oak tree grows and loves to wave
  Where Alice plucked the flowers of yore,
The wild bird sings above her grave,
  And she hath gone for evermore.

LILY-CROWNED MAY.

O hail, lovely May! fair lily crowned May!
With blossoms so sweet thou strewest the way ;
The cuckoo doth greet thee at early morn,
The blackbird sings sweetly on blooming thorn,
The daisy doth spread its silvery shield,
The golden king-cup adorneth the field,
And huge snowy wreaths of sweet hawthorn bloom
Deck the hedge-row, and the breezes perfume.
As I woo thee, fair May, on the rustic stile,
Butterflies sport on the south wind the while,
The bee on thy gems is passing the hours—
Living alone on the sweets of the flowers.
Then hail! lovely May ! fair lily-crowned May,
Thy kirtle is trimm'd with flowerets gay.

EDITH OF LEA.

Ye murmuring elms, in the woodlands of Lea,
 Wail to the oaks of the forest a dirge,
Like the sound of waves ou the shores of the sea,
 Bathing the gray rocks in showers of surge

Quiver, ye aspens, by brooklet and river,
 Tremble for Edith, the loved one of Lea!
Her troubles are o'er, she sleepeth for ever,
 Where sorrow comes not that falleth to me.

In the cottage she dwelt, was sunshine and love,
 When in the sweet charms of childhood arrayed,
She roamed the gay woodland where murmured the dove,
 And sunbeams and wild birds around the cot played.

The cottage was homely, its roof was of thatch,
 Such dwellings are hastening fast to decay,
Where wall-flowers bloom, and the daises, a batch
 Of gems, live and smile the long summer day.

It stood in the sunshine, a heaven below,
 And near to it waved a huge forest tree,
By the front of its door a brooklet did flow,
 And murmured its peaceful minstrelsy.

The brooklet was crossed by a rude wooden bridge,
 'Tangled with brambles and woodbine with grace,
It led to the cot, on whose uppermost ridge
 Flourished the house-leek as king of the place.

The home of contentment, of plenty, and peace,
 Was Edith's snug cottage, a lovelier maiden
Ne'er rambled by streamlet when cold winds cease,
 Or strayed o'er the mead with wild flowers laden.

The days of her childhood all swiftly had gone,
 She stood in the pride of maidenhood's grace,
When Edwin, enamoured, was gazing upon
 The virtuous blush that played on her face.

A God-fearing mother had trained her in youth,
   And framed each sentence that fell from her lips;
Yea, fair was the maiden, and lovely in truth
   As woodland violet from which the dew drips.

In the evenings of summer she sat 'neath the tree,
   That waved in its freedom, high o'er her head;
There waiting for Edwin, her lover, was she,
   And clustering roses their perfume shed.

And there in the twilight she knitted and sung,
   Or thoughtfully roamed the woodland serene,
Till the stars in the heavens, like silver lamps hung,
   And the moon lent its light to gladden the scene.

And ah! in that cottage, when evenings were cold,
   How swift flew the time, and sweet was the song!
And Edith would blush as the village clock told
   The hour when Edwin would gladden the throng.

From Burton's gay bowers the young lover came,
   So high are its cliffs, a fair spot of earth!
To noble young Edwin, no haunt could you name
   Dear as that chateau, the place of his birth.

How fair was the evening, and sweet the perfume,
   As Edwin once wandered to Edith's cot,
Of gems white and blue that the green-bank illume
   He plucked, and the rose that bloomed on the spot.

And he made her a wreath to place on her brow,
   She stood in the moonlight, queen of the vale,
The breezes were piping so plaintive and low,
   And were answered alone by the brooklet's tale.

He impressed on her cheek the fond kiss of love,
   "To morrow shall Edith be wedded to me,
And the sun will look down and smile from above,
   And the fairest of brides, thou, maiden! shalt be.

"I will rise with the lark, be ready, my fair!
   At eight we all to the church must be gone,
I will pluck thee roses to twine on thy hair,
   Sweet blooming roses with dew drops thereon.

"I will place round thy neck this chain of fine gold,
   And this locket that bears thy lover's device;
Now retire, dear Edith, the night wind is cold,
   Nor stay thou to thank me, thy kiss will suffice.

"To his lone woodland home thy lover must go,
   Thy bright smile is with me, dearest! farewell!
To-morrow, made happy, I'll banish my woe,
   And live with my Edith, the pride of the dell.

" O shine, lovely moon, o'er fair Edith's dwelling!
And twinkle, ye stars, o'er mountain and down!
As the rills swell the brook, my heart it is swelling
For Edith, fair maiden; then let the world frown.

" But here is the path that leads to the river,
'Neath hoary elms heavenward towering,
Here pensively ripples the Trent for ever,
And willows o'erhang its waters embowering.

" Sweet stream that windeth thro' meadow and wildwood
On thy peaceful banks once more I recline;
Sweep by, ye sprites, from the visions of childhood,
And gambol, ye nymphs, in the pale moonshine!

" Fancy's eye sees you by bright fays attended,
Bathing your limbs in Trent's cooling tide,
On its smooth surface your car is suspended—
The salmon your charger, how swiftly you glide!

" Away with such visions, they please me not now,
I'll run down the bank, and take of the flood—
O health-giving water! how cool to the brow!
'Tis life to the flowers, and health to the blood.

" And now, peaceful Trent! whose broad waters calm
Feeding the brooklets through meadows, here stray,
How sweetly ye sing your exquisite psalm
Ye waters, that ever on soft lutes play!

" The great Thames, with its woods that wave to the breeze,
It oft hath delighted its thousands of men,
But sweet Trent, on thy banks, the old willow trees
Have sheltered the mavis, blackbird, and wren.

" And the blossoming palm bends over thy stream,
The primroses pale thy green banks adorn,
And the lark with its song awakes from their dream
The milk-maid, cuckoo, and rosy-cheeked morn.

" But the season hath passed, and summer is here—
Sweet summer so young, so rosy and fair!
'Tis night, and each flower is wet with a tear,
The choicest I'll pluck to deck Edith's hair."

And, as he arose, the young herbage gave way
Quickly, he fell and was lost unto sight,
The waters closed on him and rippled away,
All nature was hushed! 'twas silent night.

And bright rose the sun o'er the high woods of Lea,
Nature was wearing its loveliest smile,
As her dear woodland home resounded with glee,
Edith awaited her lover the while.

But Edwin came not, and Edith was sad,
  And lonely she wept the long hours away,
And that beautiful form that once was so glad,
  The cankerworm, grief, had marked for its prey.

Cold frosty-locked winter was coming apace
  When Edith was borne away to the tomb,
Though her fate was hard, she had finished her race,
  But Edwin's was wrapp'd in mysterious gloom.

How fickle our joys are, how transient our bliss!
  We pluck the blossom so fragrant and fair!
And as unto our lips we press it to kiss,
  Sharp thorns reward us with pain for our care.

'Twas thus with fair Edith, who fixed her heart
  On Edwin the stalwart—blame her who dare—
On the eve of their bliss, what hand sent the dart,
  And held to that maid the cup of despair.

Yea, unto that power, all flesh must succumb,
  Then come let us learn the secret of love
From Edith, who went so young to the tomb,
  Hoping till death, and true as the dove.

Quiver, ye aspens, by brooklet and river!
  A dirge for Edith, the loved one of Lea;
Her troubles are o'er, she sleepeth for ever,
  Where sorrow comes not that falleth to me.

TO THE MORNING.

Morning fair, in radiant streams,
Sol cheers the earth with golden beams
And takes the dew-drops from the flowers,
And chases gloom from distant towers.
When the shepherd leaves his home,
To count the sheep that careless roam,
And the milk-maid in her glee,
Chants her morning minstrelsy,
And the lark with choral power
Cheereth nature's sweetest hour,
Then Aurora, in her beauty,
Calleth man from sleep to duty,
Waving us in times of olden
Her lovely banners rosy-golden.

A GLIMPSE OF THE MOUNT.

My fancy strayed one summer night
    When everything was still,
And far ahead a brilliant light
    Was shining on a hill.

And when I reached that famous hill,
    Up it I dared not climb,
So sat me down with right good will,
    To list the brooklet's rhyme.

Far up there stood among the flowers,
    In the elysian grove,
A temple with ten lofty towers,
    Built by the sons of Jove.

And on each tower a golden throne,
    On which a monarch sate,
On every lovely brow there shone
    A sapphire coronet !

And on the tenth and highest tower,
    Apollo sat arrayed,
And held a harp of thrilling power,
    Jove's lightnings round him played.

And o'er each silver tower there hung
    A rainbow in its prime,
And a thousand harps and voices sung—
    'Tis poesy's golden clime.

And in the elysian grove there strayed
    The choristers of God,
A crown divine their heads arrayed.
    They on the earth had trod.

The mount below the grove was strewn
    With briers, rocks, and thorns,
Through these the bard his way had hewn,
    And fame his head adorns.

And on the mountain's rugged side
    Some stones are placed to tell,
Where Chatterton so young had died
    And sweetest Kirk White fell.

And gazing from the mountain fair,
    I saw rush through the crowd,
A lovely youth with streaming hair—
    Before the mount he bowed.

A rude harp on his arm was slung,
    And when he reached the rocks,
He sweetly of life's troubles sung,
    Then shook his raven locks.

And climbed again, I heard him sigh,
    His bleeding limbs were torn,
His cheeks were pale, but ah ! his eye
    Was like the rising morn !

He fainted on the mountain's side,
    His rude harp from him fell,
The muse to his assistance hied,
    Apollo came as well.

They raised him to a mossy seat,
    The zephyrs fanned his head,
A maid, the youthful bard did greet,
    Returned his harp and said :—

" Take back, and sweep this harp of thine,
    Its silence gives me pain,
A thousand hearts await like mine,
    To thrill at every strain.

" Fall, melting chords, like gentle rain !
    Take courage, never fear !
" O strike thy tuneful harp, dear swain,
    Sing like the brooklet here.

O take it now, do not discard
    Thy rude strung thrilling lyre,
Apollo waits to crown thee, bard,
    Then onward ever higher."

He took his harp and sung again,
    And dashed his locks aside,
And climbed the mount, till, out of ken,
    His harp alone replied.

And he has reached the pearly gate
    Of the elysian grove,
And wanders in that grand estate,
    And temple owned by Jove.

There, free as any forester,
    He sings his lofty rhyme,
He is the chosen chorister
    Of poesy's golden clime.

TO MY LYRE.

Be hushed my sweet lyre
　　And let there be peace,
Thy soul-thrilling wire
　　And music must cease.
Alone and neglected
　　Then hang on the wall,
Despised and rejected
　　By me and by all!

For early offending
　　In silence atone,
Some think I'm depending
　　On thee, harp, alone.
They'd have thee be broken
　　And shattered and still,
Pointed at as a token
　　That's silenced at will.

Let them break every wire,
　　And treat thee with guile,
While I love thee, lyre,
　　There's one heart to smile.
As thy strings I am sweeping,
　　My sick child, God love it,
Its mother is keeping
　　Her vigils above it.

As I write at the table,
　　Though it may be wrong,
My foot on the cradle
　　Keeps time to its song ;
But its inmate's departed,
　　I cannot but weep,
When, nigh broken-hearted,
　　Thy rude strings I sweep.

Though hot tears may blind me,
　　I'll wipe them away,
And take thee, harp, kindly,
　　And sweep thee for aye.
O I love thee, my lyre !
　　Thy music I hear,
And the strains of thy wire
　　Some lone heart will cheer.

TWILIGHT.

Written on visiting L——, in June, 1866, after an absence
of nine years.

Now pensive twilight stealeth o'er the meads,
The hushed wind gently pipeth on the reeds,
The silent bats around the ruins play,
The moth and beetle sweep along their way,
The bleating lamb, suspicious of some harm,
Hies to its dam as I approach the farm,
The straying cattle, as they crop the grass,
Now murmur faintly as I near them pass.
With joy they leave the confines of the fold,
To wander in the fields of green and gold.
'Tis sweet to leave monopoly and strife,
The narrow dens and haunts of human life,
To ramble in the meads, where may be seen
The bashful lovers straying o'er the green ;
The lovely hawthorn spreads its fragrant wreath
On every hedge-row that they stray beneath,
And at each kissing-gate or rustic stile,
He pays his tribute to her sweet lips, while
The coy maid makes the peaceful woodland ring
With all the witchery that love can bring.
The merry cuckoo, as I pass along,
Chanteth its prelude to the night-birds' song ;
The quail at intervals its voice will blend,
And softly on the flowers the dews descend.
Awhile set free from every busy care,
To breathe the sweet and tranquil twilight air ;
But where is Ruth, who all the summer long,
Was wont to wake the woodland with her song ?
How oft her strains my languid soul would cheer,
'Tis scarce ten summers since she lingered here,
And though the breezes murmur as of yore,
That lovely little maid I hear no more.
With sloe-black eyes and trusting tender heart,
Fair lily of the meads must thou depart ?
Adieu, sweet Ruth, who sank beneath her yoke—
A rosebud plucked, a tender leaflet broke,
And swept away by life's cold ruthless wind,
And left to languish by the blast unkind.
'Tis early June, and round the cottage door,
The woodbine climbeth now as heretofore,

And sheds its fragrance on the evening wind,
Endearing twilight to the troubled mind.
How dear to me is such a tranquil hour,
When nature seems awhile resigning power ;
With half-shut eye, she seems to woo repose—
How like the slumb'ring child, or dew-bent rose,
That softly sleeps so peaceful for awhile,
Then opes its eyes, and spreads its leaves, to smile.
I hear fair Jenny tripping from the farm—
God shield thee, maid, from every worldly harm !
She hears the wicket-gate, that well-known sound,
And comes to meet me with a merry bound.
I hail with joy her rustic home once more,
With wall-flowers blooming ; on each side the door
The lilac waves, likewise the luscious vine
Doth here and there about the building twine,
As though they knew and loved each dear old face,
And lent their charms to beautify the place.
Ye who would learn the mysteries of peace,
Must to the woodland, where your troubles cease,
And you will find the mystic charmer there—
No wealth could lure me from a scene so fair :
Unto my heart its very air is bliss—
Adieu, calm twilight !—now for Jenny's kiss.

———

WHAT IS THE ECHO ?

O WHAT is the echo? some fairy, or sprite,
That mocketh our laughter in tones of delight ?
We call, and it speaks from its home on the hills,
Its music is sweeter than murmuring rills.
When the night winds were hushed, and breathing no
        sound,
And all nature was wrapp'd in silence profound,
I have sung till the hills have answered my strain,
Like a voice behind me it sounded so plain.
O echo sublime, where dost thou inherit ?
Reverberate sound or ærial spirit !
Thy numbers are peaceful, so softly they flow,
And whisper sweet music to mortals below.

THE BLOSSOMING BILBERRY TREE.

THE morning is fair, and the moor
　Is clad in its vestments of gold,
And the rose that blooms by my door,
　Has outlived the storm and the cold.
My Edwin's away at the plough,
　And the blackbird is piping to me,
As alone I am milking the cow,
　By the blossoming bilberry tree.

When Edwin and I went to church,
　From the dear little cot on the green,
The mavis was leaving its perch,
　As he kissed me and called me his queen.
We rested awhile on the way,
　And he kissed me again in his glee,
And his lips were as sweet as the may,
　Or the bloom on the bilberry tree.

And when his week's labour was o'er,
　We were called by the sage sabbath bell,
Through the fields we had rambled of yore,
　To the ivy-clad church in the dell.
And we listened the tale of the dove,
　And the song of the musical bee,
And he decked my brow, did my love,
　With the bloom of the bilberry tree.

Our cottage is lowly and clean,
　And the house-leek grows on its roof,
That Edwin's industrious been
　The flourishing farm is a proof.
He has nursed the children with care,
　And he sung as they sat on his knee,
And said each in its turn was as fair
　As the bloom on the bilberry tree!

My daughters have won me renown,
　They honour the man at the plough,
And look on the fop with a frown—
　But there—I have finished the cow.
I'll to the old cottage away,
　For there they are waiting for me,
And I'll pluck each loved one a spray
　From the blossoming bilberry tree.

AN INVITATION.

COME, boys, and away!
'Tis now dawn of day,
The sun is climbing up the sky.
Within the bowers,
We'll cull the flowers,
And chase the lovely butterfly.

Hark! do you not hear,
In the covert near,
The blackbird welcoming the day?
And a song of love
Now falls from above—
'Tis the skylark's thrilling lay.

With haste let us stray
To woodlands away,
The cuckoo is singing with joy,
Quick, leap ye the stile,
Now young spring doth smile
Upon you, a rosy-cheeked boy.

The jubilant thrush
Now sings in the bush,
And the cowslip blooms on the mead,
We'll rest on the moss,
The brooklet we'll cross,
And glance at the bulrush and reed.

With music of spring,
The woodland doth ring,
We will shout because we are free,
Ere brows that are fair
Are wrinkled with care,
Or we strange to liberty be.

THE TEMPERANCE STAR.

O HAVE you not heard of the temperance star,
   That shineth so steady and bright,
The isles in the sea, the nations afar,
   Have gazed on its beautiful light.
      O see how it twinkles afar!
         Its rays pure and free,
         Are shining for thee—
   . O gaze on the temperance star.

It shines o'er the homes of the pure and the free,
   Who drink of the streamlet so clear,
It waiteth to shine, poor drunkard, on thee—
   O sinner thy dark path 'twill cheer.
      O see how it twinkles afar!
         Its rays pure and free,
         Are shining for thee—
   O gaze on the temperance star.

Where rocks and quicksands are hidden below,
   'Tis placed like a beacon in love,
To save thee from ruin, and lend thee its glow
   To light thee to heaven above.
      O see how it twinkles afar!
         Its rays pure and free,
         Are shining for thee—
   O gaze on the temperance star.

THE STREAMLET.

O LET me drink of streamlet clear,
   That murmurs gently through the land,
That slakes the thirst of bounding deer,
   Fresh from its Creator's hand.

The streamlet I delight to view,
   My woodland cot it murmurs by,
Purling water, crystal dew,
   That sparkles in the floweret's eye!

I love to see it pure and bright,
   Babbling in the little rill,
Or rushing from its mountain height—
   Of water let me take my fill.

THE EAST MAY BOAST.

THE East may boast of orange bloom,
  Of cypress and of laurel,
And we will boast of yellow broom,
  Of orchards rich and floral.
Eastern blooms and foliage fair,
  Are of the rainbow's dapple,
In England blossom everywhere
  The pear, the plum, and apple.
      Then boast who will
        Of trees in spring array,
      Albion still
        Hath blossoms fair as they.

The East may boast of citron tree,
  That yields so fair a flower,
Our lilac's sweeter on the lea,
  When freshened by a shower.
They boast of lemon and of pine,
  We of our mellow cherry,
They of their spice and juicy wine,
  And we our luscious berry.
      Then boast who will
        Of trees and fruit so gay,
      Albion still
        Hath fruit as sweet as they.

SONNET.

AND art thou gone at last, my little child!
  No more to cheer me with thy loving smile,
  Freed from the world before thou knew its guile;
Then why, my heart be torn with anguish wild?
Sleep on sweet child, no more the soft caress
  Shall wake thee from that long and peaceful sleep,
  O'er thee thy mother may her vigils keep,
And kiss thy cold lips in her sore distress.
Now on thy spirit's sight hath burst a scene
  Thou wouldst not quit for this thy earthly home!
Too long thy soul hath in its prison been—
  Go, then, sweet child, and with the angels roam!
Thy spirit longed to leave its tent of clay,
And quit this vale of want and woe for aye.

IMPROMPTU

On seeing a blackbird shot while singing on an old thorn-
tree behind my cottage at Horncastle.

SWEET, gentle warbler cease to sing,
And fly upon thy glossy wing
    To some lone vale or grot,
From orchestra of rugged thorn
    Behind my little cot,
Where thou hast welcomed rosy morn.

Or soon I shall lament thy death
In tears, what makes me hold my breath ?
    That sudden flash of flame,
Thee falling from that lofty height,
    Besmeared with gore, and lame—
My heart is sad at such a sight.

Alas ! poor struggling, tuneful thing !
Men treat us thus : if we would sing
    Both bird and bard must pay,
The man whose eye hath sighted thee,
    His ears be deaf, O ! may
That eye ne'er gaze on bird or tree !

MY COT SHALL BE THE HOME OF THE FREE.

WHERE the huge rocks frown on the deep below,
    And the sea-gull mounts on high,
And the crags are tinged with the sunset glow,
    That now gilds the western sky,
My cot shall be the home of the free,
        Where the breakers dash,
        And the gray-rocks splash,
And mermaids chant their minstrelsy.

How I love to climb the high cliffs and hills
    In the happy summer time,
And to list to the merry dancing rills,
    That are babbling forth their rhyme !
My cot shall be the home of the free,
        Where the breaker raves,
        In the rocky caves,
And mermaids chant their minstrelsy.

SPRING.

FLORA comes with crown of flowers,
  In her hand the plenteous horn,
To reside in sylvan bowers,
  Till Ceres reaps the golden corn.
With sweet flowers she decks the vale,
  And clothes the trees with bursting buds,
Spreads lilies and the primrose pale
  In happy clusters through the woods.

The gentle south winds glide along,
  And with her blossoms strew the ground,
Her warbling choir with gladsome song,
  Makes wood and grove and hill resound.
She looks upon the ice-bound lakes,
  They melt beneath her tender glance,
The silver ripple she awakes
  To pipe its gentle eloquence.

She mounts above the misty shrouds,
  That hang about in winter's reign,
With rainbow tints she paints the clouds,
  And bids the zephyr fan the swain.
Then ever welcome, lovely spring,
  With flowery robes and joyous lays !
Come swiftly on thy downy wing,
  Sweet messenger of sunny days !

THE LAUGH OF THE CHILDREN FOR ME.

THERE'S grandeur in watching the billow,
  And hearing the voice of the seas,
There's music so soft in the willow,
  When swept by the whispering breeze.

And music the soul can inspire,
  Its cords the spirit can heal;
As he toucheth the strings of his lyre,
  What pleasure the poet must feel !

There's Bacchus, and jolly faced mirth,
  A couple bewitching and free,
But of all the pleasures on earth,
  The laugh of the children for me.

EVENING.

Evening! sweet hour when nature sleeps,
And every blushing floweret weeps,
When wailing boughs to peace are hushed,
Where'er the chill wild winds have gushed,
When crimson clouds are tinged with gray,
Night spreads its curtain round the day,
And in the eve at twilight's hush,
We hear the last strain of the thrush
Come sounding o'er the verdant plain,
To cheer the heart of every swain,
Who weary from his toil returns,
Welcomed by her whose fond heart burns
With love for him she can admire—
To do his will's her sole desire.
And children that can scarcely prate
They run to meet him at the gate.
Here peace spreads out its mystic wings,
And brooding o'er us faintly sings!
How calm and loved are scenes like this,
Wooing the heart to dreams of bliss!
O for a heart to beat with mine,
Pure as a beam of light divine!
To roam o'er meadows, sit by streams,
Lost in the muse's pensive dreams,
And to enjoy the calm that thou,
Sweet evening! shed'st around thee now!
And to behold the peaceful scene
Where folly's noisy laugh hath been;
To roam the hills and lovely vales,
And feel the freshness of their gales.
And while these thoughts my mind employ,
And make me feel an inward joy,
The day on silent wings hath flown,
Like a blast from some trumpet blown,
Whose echoes die upon the hill,
And bid the noise of man be still.
A song now breaks the tranquil sleep,
In cadence rich from thicket deep
The nightingale, when all is mute,
Breathes forth her notes to mock the lute—
This bird, sweet minstrel of the night,
In covert dim sings far from sight,

Its modulations are of peace,
But Muta bids the songster cease.
A death-like stillness reigns around,
No voice is heard, nor yet a sound,
Save in the distance, far behind,
The bleat of sheep borne on the wind,
The owl and night-bird's dreary scream,
The plaintive murmur of the stream;
While to the breeze the branches sing
A dirge and close my evening.

———

TO SCARBOROUGH.

SCARBORO' to thy scenes united,
   Never from thee would I roam,
With thy rocks and waves delighted,
   Let me ever call thee home.

Fate decreed that we should sever,
   Yet 'tis only for awhile,
I would not leave thy haunts for ever,
   Though fortune would upon me smile.

Though thy waves in mournful numbers
   Oft have told how sad my lot,
Still in my heart their music slumbers,
   Nor are thy lovely scenes forgot.

To thee alone my love is plighted,
   Thoughts fly to thee evermore,
To where my young heart was delighted
   On the cliffs that gird thy shore.

The star of hope, through sorrow beaming,
   Bids me brave each strife and ill,
Through storm and sunshine of thee dreaming,
   Scarbro' let me love thee still.

And when age my frame hath shattered,
   Then would I linger by the deep,
And o'er my corse, the earth all scattered,
   In thy grave-yard I would sleep.

To thy lovely scenes united,
   Never from thee would I roam,
With thy rocks and waves delighted,
   Let me ever call thee home.

AMALGAMATION.

HARK! freedom's trump proclaims, ye sad
And weary hearts once more be glad,
A banner waves o'er land and sea,
The words engraven on it be,—
                              Amalgamation.

Now hand in hand, and heart in heart,
Let every workman take a part
To raise the banner high in air,
And let each breast the motto bear—
                              Amalgamation.

" Unity we find is power,"
By the scent we know the flower,
Hearts united nought can sever,
Workmen be united ever—
                              Amalgamation.

Toil and trouble, bravely bear it,
Win the crown then you shall wear it,
And raise that care-worn, drooping brow—
Hark! freedom's voice proclaimeth now
                              Amalgamation.

Though rough the road, press onward still,
And face the conflict, brave the ill,
Then tyrant foes shall melt away,
Like mists before the orb of day—
                              Amalgamation.

All vice and folly leave behind,
And ever seek to be refined!
Mark the snowdrops bloom together,
Thriving in the stormy weather—
                              Amalgamation.

And in these snowdrops may we see
The secret of true unity,
And let us raise the banner high,
Extol its motto to the sky—
                              Amalgamation.

OUR JOYS ARE BRIEF.

Our life is a season of sweet smiles and tears,
We have bright hopes to-day, to-morrow sad fears,
And our joys are as brief as the sun's brightest ray,
Soon dark clouds o'ershadow and hide them away.
They have wings like the wind, and swift is their flight,
They flit from our grasp ere we feel their delight,
Their stay is as brief as the hail on the ground,
For soon it dissolveth and cannot be found.
White fleecy clouds like to silver are seen,
To float 'neath the heavens when the air is serene;
But storms soon appear their beauty to blight,
So the earth's sweetest joy soon taketh its flight.
Here troubles beset us—yet all is not strife,
Our joys are as flowers in the pathway of life,
But at best they are brief, they flee as our breath,
And oft are the highways to sorrow and death :
They fly as the seasons, like spring with its showers,
When cometh the summer unfolding its flowers,
To give place to autumn, ah! then fades the leaf—
Remember, O mortal! thy joys are as brief.

TO MISS E. P——.

Of life, fair maiden, art thou weary ?
  Shines there no star to light the way ?
Hath the world become a desert dreary ?
  Droops the floweret to decay ?

And hath it gone, the blush of beauty ?
  That tinged thy cheek with rosy hue ;
And is it now the muse's duty ?
  Then breathe it softly forth—adieu !

Yes, they have gone, the days of childhood,
  Youth with all its sunny hours,
When we roamed the pleasant wildwood,
  Plucking, as we strayed, the flowers.

How the memory fain would linger
  On that bright and happy shore,
Pointing with its mystic finger,
  To the scenes we loved of yore.

Then, maiden, if the spell be broken
  That bound our hearts—yet who can tell ?
These lines may be the heartfelt token
  Of a humble bard's farewell.

THE STAR OF FREEDOM.

Written on the passing of the Reform Bill of 1867.

THE star of freedom shines this morning,
    Workman, only wait awhile,
Fearless every danger scorning,
    Then on you its light will smile.
Now a ray of brighter glory
    In the distance we may scan,
Proclaiming still the ancient story, .
    Peace and brotherhood to man!

Light of freedom doth it render,
    While the workman poet sings ;
Of its blessings and its splendour,
    We only catch the glimmerings.
Though to-day its face be shrouded,
    Workmen never think of sorrow,
It only for awhile is clouded,
    To shine more brightly on the morrow.

Though in narrow chamber moaning,
    A ray of hope it sheds for thee,
Though beneath oppression groaning,
    Thou'rt on the eve of liberty !
Workmen wait a little longer,
    The light in lustrous floods appears,
Every moment growing stronger,
    Then cease to sigh and dry thy tears.

Shine, bright star, on hearts now grieving,
    In rustic cot or rented room !
Where'er a workman's breast is heaving,
    Let thy rays dispel his gloom !
Illumine all the little bowers,
    Where dwells the strength of Britain's bride,
O shine, fair star, till like the flowers,
    We dwell as peaceful side by side !

WILSON'S WOOD VALLEY.

OR, CAST OFF THY SORROW.

In Wilson's wood valley, one bright summer day,
A linnet sat singing, and sweet was its lay.
I was silent and sad, repining in grief,
The song of the bird to my heart brought relief.
And what soft notes of love the bird had to say,
As on the green furze it carolled away !
Though the world on thee frown, and keen is thy care,
From thy noble heart tear the thorn of despair,
And cast off thy sorrow, why weepest thou here ?
Yes, nature will yield thee some joy for that tear ;
Some wreath is being twined from green laurel tree,
And honours undreamt of are waiting for thee.
Though violets have gone, and primroses pale,
Still some rich gems adorn sweet Wilson's wood vale —
Here the hare-bell doth droop, the speedwell doth grow,
The willow-wort springs from the streamlet below.
Wildroses blooming, the brambles in flower ;
The marjoram's scent is perfuming the bower.
Round the stems of the trees the green ivy clings,
And the sea on thy vision its majesty flings.
Then cease thy repining, there's sunshine above,
The greenwoods are ringing with sweet songs of love—
Are all ringing for thee; then hush thy plaint wail,
And sing of the beauties of Wilson's wood vale.

Scarboro', July, 1865.

STANZAS

On a Primrose found on the South Cliffs, Scarboro', Jan. 13, 1866

Sweet primrose, I plucked it from yon sunny nook,
  On the cliffs where I've oft been a ranger,
'Neath a flowering furze that grows by a brook,
  It was hid from the gaze of the stranger.

At the bright glimpse of morn it opens to view,
  And its sweet woodland fragrance discloses,
In the evening it bends its head to the dew,
  And on green leaves its pale form reposes.

Pale herald of spring, the bright little flower,
  That was bidding us cast away sadness,
It was blooming to cheer us in sorrow's dim hour,
  And forestalling the season of gladness.

In its snug little home, on the high cliffs there,
  It bloomed when the storm was up-springing,
The primrose is here, then cast aside care,
  And the blackbird is joyfully singing.

THE FALSE AND THE TRUE.

A PRIMROSE bloomed on a lofty height,
   And a young bard saw it there,
And his heart did pant with a strange delight
   To reach that gem so fair.

And up he rose at the morning's blush,
   And his step was firm and fast,
And he climbed the crag till the twilight's hush
   Proclaimed that the day was past.

And the little flower before him lay,
   When arose a bitter blast,
And the ruthless wind swept the gem away,
   And the bard below was cast.

But he rose again with a joyful heart,
   As another caught his view,
And soon the young bard resolved to start,
   And strive for the good and true.

And up he has gone with an eagle's flight,
   The first gem he saw was fame,
But the last one was love, and by its light
   He has left a deathless name.

STANZAS.

The following lines were sent in reply to a letter I received
from a Lady, who desired to know, "how I could write
verse, and suffer so much privation."

   I PASS through life like other men,
      That toil and stray,
   Save dropping leaflets now and then
      Upon the way.

   When calumny, with poisoned tongue,
      My name did blast,
   I took my harp and sweetly sung,
      And so it past.

   I've seen the forest monarch torn,
     . And blighted lay,
   Its foliage and branches borne
      By winds away—

   All in a mass of ruin lay,
     Dear lady friend ;
   "Life's roughest storm will pass away,"
     If we will bend.

THE CUCKOO.

The frost has gone, the pelting rain,
Old winter, with his bitter train ;
That welcome bird sings on the plain—
     The Cuckoo.

She comes when balmy breezes blow,
And smoothly all the streamlets flow,
With dulcet voice so sweet and low—
     The Cuckoo.

Her home is on the verdant lea,
And as she flits from tree to tree,
She sings a song for you and me—
     'Tis Cuckoo.

She riseth ere the day is born,
And shouting, hails the blush of morn,
When sparkling dew is on the thorn--
     The Cuckoo.

I hear her on the gentle gale,
At twilight, as I walk the vale,
The notes that do my ear assail,
     Are Cuckoo.

She comes when balmy breezes blow,
And smoothly all the streamlets flow,
With dulcet voice so sweet and low—
     The Cuckoo.

———

COME ROAM WITH ME.

Come, come, and roam with me, my lass !
Come when the dew is on the grass !
Come when the gentle zephyrs sigh !
Come when the stars light up the sky !

Come, love, unto the vale's retreat !
Come when the rose is blushing sweet !
Come where the scented woodbine twines !
Come in the eve when day declines !

Come, love, with me to yonder grove,
And rest thee in the sweet alcove,
Where blue-bells droop, the stream runs free,
And murmurs music pleasantly !

Come when the moon sails high above,
And let us tell sweet tales of love,
And we shall hear the night-bird sing,
And make the shady covert ring.

Then come, and roam with me, my lass !
Come when the dew is on the grass !
Come when the leaf-clad branches sigh,
And shining gems bedeck the sky !

THE RED FLAG WAVES.

Addressed to the Journeymen Tailors of London, June, 1867.

THE red flag waves, ye gallant band !
Be truth your motto, hand in hand,
Firm beneath your banner stand,
    Or yield and be
The slaves of wealth, in this fair land
    Of liberty.

Methinks no man on earth could yield—
With live and let live on his shield,
The sword of truth, and right to wield,
    When he is free,
If such a craven stains our field,
    Slave may he be.

Long have you toiled, alas ! for years,
And down your pale cheeks scalding tears
Have chased each other, and your fears
    Have long been great ;
Now mammon, laughing at you, rears
    A proud estate.

Then toil no more till you can reap
The fruits of honest toil, and keep
Long-faced hunger in the deep
    Of lethe's wave,
Nor pine away no more, nor weep
    Ye martyrs brave !

If mammon will not hear, God must,
And give you what is right and just,
And take from boastful mammon's trust
    The spoil of years—
'Tis not God's will you earn your crust
    In pain and tears.

Our union's wealth hath sought to crush,
And break up as a slender rush,
With deeds that made " the angels blush "
    To look upon—
Let freedom's fire our pale cheeks flush
    Ere we are gone.

I

This mammon let us brave like men,
And hurl his threatening back again,
And scorn for aye the filthy den
    Where we were caged
From sunshine and from mortal ken —
    My soul's enraged !

And calls upon you not to fly,
But stand and face the enemy,
And shout, and wave the red flag high—
    Jove loves to see
The honest soldier fight and die
    For liberty.

On, workman ! on, the battle's ours,
The red flag waves from all our towers,
The tyrant yields, and all his powers
    Are scattered—see !
Your conquering heads are crowned with flowers
    And victory.

THE DYING GIRL'S VISION.

MOTHER! see the angels yonder !
    Hark ! they breathe a holy song,
I hear the music, as I ponder,
    Wafted from the spirit throng.
Spirits bright that dwell above !
Let me learn that song of love !

Numbers are the throng increasing,
    Now a host repeats the strain,
They are my fettered soul releasing
    From its earthly prison-chain.
Take me, O ye spirits bright !
To the realms of love and light.

Christ, the holy one, is bleeding—
    Hark ! he groans ! for me he dies ;
He with God is interceding
    For my passport to the skies.
Spirits bright that dwell above !
Let me join your song of love !

Now my lips begin to quiver,
    Mother, take your parting kiss !
I die, then death is but the giver
    Of life immortal, holy bliss !
Take me, O ye spirits bright !
To those lovely realms of light.

A BOY TO A ROBIN.

Art thou singing, little robin,
  When all is lone and drear,
And I have no crumbs to give thee—
  What makes thee warble here?
Start not, sweet bird, I'll harm thee not—
  On many a winter's day,
Thou hast sat upon that thorn-bush
  To charm me with thy lay.

Then sing away, sweet robin,
  When all is lone and drear,
Though I have nought to give thee,
  I love thy warbling here!
How oft about our cottage,
  With crumbs I've strewn the floor,
To entice thee, little songster,
  Into my mother's door.

Though the rich and proud pass by us,
  And care not for our cot,
Yet me and thee, O robin!
  We love the dear old spot.
Though not so great as they are,
  We are, sweet bird, as free,
And freedom, love, and friendship,
  They have a charm for me.

They seem to teach my boyish mind
  That men should brothers be,
Should brave the ills in life's lone path,
  And sing, dear bird, like thee;—
But what makes thee sing, I know not,
  When all is lone and drear,
And I have no food to give thee,
  Yet thou art welcome here.

Ah! my only little sister,
  She loved to see thee fly;
When she had no food to give thee,
  She'd sit her down and cry.
Dost thou miss the maiden, robin?
  She lies among the dead—
Will thou sing upon the hawthorn,
  That grows above her head?

                              Dec. 1858.

O, I WOULD BE A BUTTERFLY.

O, I would be a butterfly,
  To flit from flower to flower,
To have a home in every nook,
  In every hedge a bower.

My dwelling in the sunshine,
  When cooling breezes blow,
To live along in chrysalis,
  When falls the winter's snow.

To flutter on the south wind,
  The live-long summer day,
And rest upon the wild-rose,
  That blossoms by the way.

To dwell amongst the perfume,
  In every sunny clime,
To creep into the flowers,
  And dream away the time,

O, I would be a butterfly,
  To flit from flower to flower,
To have a home in every nook,
  In every hedge a bower.

THE ZEPHYR-KISSED GEM.

The zephyr-kissed gem on the banks of the Bane
  Was blooming so fragrant and fair,
The purple-eyed thing had just sipt of the rain,
    And lent us its perfume so rare :
  The zephyr-kissed gem, the zephyr-kissed gem,
  Fair Flora then wore on her diadem.

By the Bane there's a gem, for me has a charm,
  Like the flower untainted with guile,
As she blushingly tripped away from the farm,
    She captured my heart with her smile.
  This zephyr-kissed gem, this zephyr-kissed gem,
  My fond heart now wears as its diadem.

SUMMER.

WHEN the mists, in fitful hazes,
　Disappear before the sun,
And the stream through thousand mazes
　On its course doth smoothly run.
When the wooobine in the morning,
　With its scent perfumes the air,
And leaflets are the boughs adorning
　In the greenwood everywhere.
Then is rosy summer gay,
Dancing on the new-mown hay,
Then the mower's voice is heard,
And the creaking meadow-bird.

When the floral gems are bending
　Gently to the balmy breeze,
And the boy his cattle tending,
　Stretched his length beneath the trees.
When the wood-doves, in the bowers,
　Sit complaining on the sprays,
And the roses, lovely flowers,
　Are opening to the sun's bright rays ;
Then is rosy summer gay,
Strewing flowers by the way,
Lovely maiden in her glee,
Chanting her sweet melody !

When the streamlet is replying
　To the linnet's plaintive song,
And in air the sky-lark flying,
　Doth her melting notes prolong—
When we wander from our dwelling,
　On a silent summer night,
Birds their evening anthems swelling,
　While the groves ring with delight ;
Then is rosy summer gay,
Dancing on the new-mown hay —
Lovely maiden in her glee,
Cheering us with melody !

When the cov'nant bow is shining,
　Clouds discharge their fruitful drops,
And the sun's last rays declining,
　Gild the distant mountain tops ;

Then the summer yields a pleasure
    That no other season can,
And we feel the floral treasure
    Elevates the soul of man.
Then is rosy summer gay,
Strewing flowers by the way—
See! the maiden in her glee,
Chanting her sweet melody!

AN AUTUMN SONG.

AUTUMN leaves are falling round us,
    Fades the grass upon the hills,
Flowerets dead that oft have bound us,
    With their breath, beside the rills.

Ceres seeks not to alarm us,
    Lingers while the sky is blue—
How her fading vestments charm us,
    Rich and beauteous in hue.

Harvest's home, and safe in garner,
    Hip and haw alike are ripe,
By the fire the homely farmer
    Chatteth o'er his glass and pipe.

Through the boughs the breeze is sighing,
    In the fields the cattle low,
Southward are the swallows flying,
    Faster doth the streamlet flow.

See! a band of maidens ramble,
    From the hamlet and the farm,
Laughing as they pluck the bramble
    From its thorny parent's arm.

Hark! the robin on the willow,
    Chants a merry autumn strain!
Soon the winds will sweep the billow,
    And the winter clothe the plain.

Autumn leaves are falling round us,
    Fades the grass upon the hills,
Flowerets dead that oft have bound us,
    With their breath, beside the rills.

DREAMLAND.

The Working Man the Bard of the Future.

Ah, once on a time I wandered away
In dreamland, by sea beaten shore did I stray,
And on the gray rocks not long had I been,
When I beheld in my vision fair Albion's Queen,
And with her a minstrel in silken attire,
Who held in his hand a rich polished lyre,
And he swept its sweet strings, and chanted a lay—
Like zephyrs in summer he softly did play!
And there by the sea side, with gray-beard so long,
The old harper stood, and he chanted a song;
So smooth were his numbers, so feeble his lay,
Her majesty wandered in dreamland away.
When a workman appeared from the factory's throng,
Whose eyes beamed with light, and whose sinews were
              strong,
He stood in his manhood when thrilled to his stroke
A harp of great sweetness, with casement of oak.
His tones were as deep as the voice of the wave,
As he bent to his harp, and sung of the brave,
Now melting to tears, and then stirring to strife,
He sang of the struggles of working-man-life.
At the soul-melting lay, and music so sweet,
Her majesty started at once to her feet,
Saying, sweep me the lyre, for plainly I see,
The workman the bard of the future will be.
The rich hoary harper no longer did frown,
But unto the workman presented his crown,
A host of great souls sat entranced on the shore,
As I woke from my dream and heard them no more.

ARISE IN THE MORNING.

Arise in the morning early,
    The skylark is soaring aloft,
The birds are awake in brier and brake,
    And their music is joyous and soft.

Arise in the morning early,
    Away to the sylvan retreat,
To where the fleet fawn doth bound o'er the lawn,
    And ringdove's are murmuring sweet.

Arise in the morning early,
   And let us roam in the bowers,
For there the sweet breeze doth sigh through the trees,
   Laden with fragrance of flowers.

Arise in the morning early,
   It is the great spring-time of health,
The cheeks are made fair by sweet morning air,
   'Tis likewise the safe road to wealth.

Arise in the morning early,
   And thy garments quickly put on,
For mark how the day is passing away !
   How soon its best moments are gone !

THE SNOW FLAKE.

It comes as silently as love,
Or like the plumage of a dove,
Descending from the clouds above —
           The snow-flake.

Pale child of air, how brief its stay,
Dissolving in the sun's bright ray,
It in the warm hand melts away—
           The snow-flake.

It adds a drop unto the sea,
And clothes with white the forest-tree,
I would mankind were pure as thee—
           O snow-flake.

We see it drifted by the wind,
Flake by flake it is combined,
Until an avalanche we find —
           Of snow-flakes.

In Alpine lands, how sad the doom
To perish in a snowy tomb !
But here it gives a pleasing gloom—
           The snow-fluke.

Kissing the sod with lips so sweet,
It finds us in the narrow street,
Yes, it is nature's winding sheet—
           The snow flake.

It softly falls when clouds are dull,
And in the air there is a lull,
So fragile and so beautiful —
           The snow-flake.

SUMMER COMES.

SUMMER comes, rejoice, rejoice !
  The apple blossom's shaking,
I hear the nightingale's rich voice,
  The doves their nests are making.
The chestnuts wave their flow'ring heads,
  The aspen banners quiver,
The lilac all its perfume sheds,
  And smoothly flows the river.

Upon its banks the willows grow,
  Their silver leaflets turning,
They bend and kiss the stream below,
  When Sol's bright beams are burning.
Laburnums hang in festoons gay,
  And fall in golden shower,
The speedwell blooms by the highway,
  A bonny blue-eyed flower.

The hawthorn on the hedge is spread,
  The buttercups bloom yellow,
Trees wave their branches overhead,
  And skims the stream the swallow.
Summer comes, rejoice, ye sad !
  The apple blossom's falling,
The linnet and the lark so glad,
  Are you from sorrow calling.

Gainsborough, June, 1866.

THE EMIGRANT'S FAREWELL TO ALBION.

FAREWELL to the home of my childhood for aye,
  The land of oppression and toil,
Where might o'er the lowly and just hath the sway,
  And the rich reap the fruits of the soil.

The land where oppressors are proud in their state,
  And serfs come and go at their call,
Where the ill-fed workman for comforts must wait—
  Until he is lord with them all.

That home in the woodland will know me no more,
  Ye friends of my childhood, adieu !
I will seek me a cot on some far distant shore,
  Where all to the workman are true.

K

Brave brothers, o'er you there hovers a friend,
 'Tis the bird whose plumage is red,
Round the world it will fly, its mission will end,
 When oppressors and tyrants are dead.

O sit thee, proud Albion, in ashes and dust,
 And repent of wrongs to thy sons,
Ere writhing in gore, down, down thou art thrust,
 Yea, in spite of thy lofty ones.

Employers have crushed me, and ruined my health,
 With troubles have chastened me sore,
I delved in my blindness to add to their wealth,
 I'll be lion's provider no more.

Ah! wonder not, sailor, to see the salt tear,
 That starts from my eye-lid so free,
In the land I leave dwells a fond mother dear,
 And the fairest of maidens to me.

Then bear me, swift barque, from her I love best,
 And boldly dash on o'er the wave,
To the land of the free in the glorious west—
 Where the fetters are cast from the slave.

THE SPEEDWELL.

When the black-thorn bloom is cast
From the hedge-row by the blast,
And the hawthorn blossoms fly,
Like the snow-flakes 'neath the sky
 Of early June, then blooms a flower;
And the blue-eyed gem appears,
Smiling through its dewy tears,
Lifting up its hopeful head
From its green and mossy bed,
 And every sunny bank and bower.

Where the waters in the brook,
Winding run from bend to nook,
There on every bank is seen,
The speedwell, in its robe of green,
 Oft braving out the bitter blast.
Dear is its wee bloom to me,
Emblem of fidelity,
In its frail and blue expanse,
Behold the child's most faithful glance,
 'Tis ever trustful to the last.

Children oft have plucked this gem
For their floral diadem,
And we see in its bright eye,
The beauty of the summer sky,
  The fragile form of man and flower ;
Crushed beneath the ploughboy's tread,
Never more to raise its head,
Scattered by the autumn wind,
Not a trace is left behind,
  Save naked stem in leafless bower.

THE HARE-BELL OF THE DOWN.

One autumn morn the sun arose,
  And shed his golden rays,
O'er verdant mead where herds repose,
  And bleating flocks do graze.
That lovely morn unto the heath
  I wandered from the town,
When, bright and blue, there caught my view
  The hare-bell of the down.

The fields were full of golden grain,
  The cool fruit on the tree,
The bramble rip'ning on the plain,
  Where hare-bells love to be.
I saw the little flower then,
  When leaves and moss were brown,
Droop on its stem, submissive gem!
  The hare-bell of the down !

The summer birds the brakes forsook,
  And early in the morn,
The robin, with its love song, shook
  The dewdrops from the thorn ;
And o'er the heath there came a maid,
  With cheeks all sunny brown,
I then did meet her smiling sweet—
  My hare-bell of the down !

I plucked the gem to deck her brow,
  But soon it faded fell,
A token frail of every vow
  We plighted in the dell.
O could I spend my days with thee,
  Then all the world might frown,
'Twere sweet to rest upon the breast,
  Sweet hare-bell of the down.

THE FIELDS THEIR EMERALD ROBES PUT ON.

THE fields their emerald robes put on,
  The thrush begins to sing,
The snowdrop blooms to greet you, John!
  The lark is on the wing.
Away all care and sorrow cast!
  Poor widow, dry that tear!
The winter with its storms hath past,
  And lovely spring is here.

The fields their emerald robes put on,
  The crocus doth appear,
The primrose blooms to greet you, John!
  The violet is here.
There's life and love in every beam
  Shed by the cheering sun,
And music sweet in every stream,
  That rippling past doth run.

The fields their emerald robes put on,
  With joy I hail the morn,
The golden furze doth greet you, John!
  The blossom's on the thorn.
She smiles on every heart and home,
  That lovely maiden, spring!
Invites me in the vale to roam,
  Where birds are carolling.

———

VIOLETS.

VIOLETS beautiful and blue,
  The green bank adorning,
  This bright sunny morning,
And all dripping with dew.
Sweet flowers! O that all could see
  You so meekly blooming,
  The zephyrs perfuming,
What eyes would gaze on ye!
The maiden that loved us so true,
  Now bashful she lingers,
  And takes from our fingers
Violets wet with dew.

Pale looking girls, with tear-dimm'd eyes,
  And sorowful faces,
  Would waft to the graces
The sad tumult of sighs.
And others would sing in their glee,
  As larks on their pinions,
  Soar o'er your dominions,
And delight to be free.
And maidens that weep 'neath care's rod,
  Would hail you, sweet flowers,
  That bloom in the bowers,
As gifts of love from God.

And children that we loved of yore,
  Would pluck you in gladness—
  But great is our sadness,
We behold them no more !
Yet flowers like you they are fair,
  For on fancy's pinions.
  We mount God's dominions,
And see our blossoms there.
Violets white, violets blue,
  The green-bank adorn,
  This fair sunny morn,
And all dripping with dew.

———

AUTUMN.

The summer is over and Ceres appears
With torch and with poppy and garland of ears,
Which were plucked in their beauty from earth's ver-
    dant glade,
'Neath the shade of the greenwood her garland was made.
The voice of the reaper is heard in the field,
All nature doth promise a bounteous yield.
See, the trees in the orchards with fruit are bent down,
And the leaves and the branches are tinted with brown.
Through yonder field, where the grain in a mass
Now waves to the breeze, a maiden doth pass
With a bottle, and basket, and humming a song,
The hard-toiling reaper hath wished for her long.
The woods they have lost their summer attire,
Yet autumn's rich vestments we all must admire,
For Ceres will charm us with rich golden tresses,
When Flora hath fled with her beautiful dresses.

In upland or dell 'tis pleasant to ramble,
When falleth the leaf, and ripe is the bramble,
When the red-breasted songster doth start from the tree
And warbles his wood-notes alone on the lea.
Hark! to the gale! through the branches it sings,
Like a hand sweeping a harp's mellow strings,
Or the voices of fairies, while dancing their round—
It speaks to the soul in a language profound.
The beauties of autumn, brown, golden, and green,
Are mild in their lustre, and tranquil in mien;
Ere winter, the flowers will be gone to decay,
And the quivering leaves will be wasted away.
How quiet is autumn, how peaceful and still!
Nature declines, saith the musical rill—
O sweet pensive season, thy loved melancholy
Refineth the mind with pure feelings so holy!

I HAVE WATCHED ALONE BY MOONLIGHT.

I HAVE watched alone by moonlight,
  And waited, love, for thee,
When the stars above me shone bright,
  O'er the wide wailing sea.
And the winds above have answered
  The strains the ocean sung,
And the high rocks o'er the waters
  Their frowning shadows hung.
I have called upon thy name, love!
  Nor did a voice reply,
Save the shrieking of the curlew,
  As it was flitting by.

I have watched alone by moonlight,
  Have seen the cattle stray,
Where the brambles ever bloom bright
  With the hare-bells by the way.
Where beneath the beech-tree branches
  The daisy may be found,
And the hare or fleet deer glances
  So timidly around.
I have listened for thy voice, love!
  Alas! I heard no lay,
Save the murmur of the wood-dove
  In coverts far away.

I have watched alone by moonlight,
  Some lowly cot my tower,
When the pearly dewdrops shone bright
  On every blushing flower!
And the little winding streamlet
  Swept merrily along,
Giving life unto the flowers,
  And murmuring its song;
And I heard in all my watches,
  In woodland or by sea,
The voice of God through nature,
  Saying, mortal learn of me!

BESIDE THE BRIGHT WATERS OF MUSICAL TRENT.

THE night-bird was singing, the soft summer breeze
Was murmuring gently through old willow trees,
As at midnight all lonely my footsteps I bent,
Beside the bright waters of musical Trent.

The sedge warblers twittered in the moonlight pale,
The smooth waters glittered like rich polished mail,
The rose to the zephyr its perfume had lent,
Beside the bright waters of musical Trent.

The anchor was lifted at opening day,
The ship from its moorings was drifting away,
And the voice of the boatman the still air rent—
Beside the bright waters of musical Trent.

Lonely I wandered, till daylight appeared,
The song of the mavis my sadness had cheered,
And the lark from on high its sweet carol sent,
Beside the bright waters of musical Trent.

The dew was adorning each floweret meek,
The sweet breath of morning was fanning my cheek,
And her blush to the sky Aurora had lent,
Beside the bright waters of musical Trent.

The fair gems of nature their beauty disclose,
The woodbine entwining was kissing the rose,
And they all on the breeze their sweetness have spent,
Beside the bright waters of musical Trent.

Flow on, ever on, O beautiful river!
Thy murmuring waters wander for ever!
Delighting the thousands whose footsteps are bent
Beside the bright waters of musical Trent.

BEAUTY WILL NOT LAST FOR AYE.

THE fragrant flower it blooms to fade,
And wither in the sylvan shade,
Its sweet perfume must pass away,
Its blossom must in ruin lay.
Nor will the foliage on the tree,
In winter grace the verdant lea,
All things must yield to stern decay,
Since beauty will not last for aye.

I saw a maiden young and fair,
With rosy cheek and auburn hair,
And o'er her did another bend,
In converse with her lovely friend.
Since Venus hath made thee her choice,
In accents like an angel's voice,
She whispering in her ear did say,—
" Thy beauty will not last for aye ! "

Time, fair beauty's cheek will blight,
The raven locks will turn to white,
The glancing eye, the tender tone,
Though like the ring-dove's gentle moan,
Be hushed in death, for thou must die,
And o'er thy grave the breeze will sigh,
Saying, as it sweeps away,
Thy beauty will not last for aye !

THE WOODLAND MAID.

IN yonder verdant valley
    The plough-boy tells his tales,
The swift-winged pigeons sally,
    And hawthorns scent the gales.
There dwelt a blue-eyed maiden,
    Whose smile the heart would cheer,
Her hair with flowers laden
    Fresh from the greenwood near.

The spring was scarcely over,
    When Hebe had to stray
Through fields of blooming clover,
    To turn the scented hay.
Oft 'neath an old oak sitting,
    When summer nights were long,
And as she plied her knitting
    Her voice broke out in song.

At morn within the bowers,
　At noon beneath the shade,
She loved to cull the flowers
　That blossomed on the glade.
Then by the brooklet straying,
　Just when the sun retires,
To hear the waters playing
　Upon their murmuring lyres.

And when the stars were beaming,
　The balmy air breathed love,
The moon through white clouds gleaming
　In the firmament above.
Ah! then she loved to ramble
　When dew was on the bloom,
She fairy-like would amble.
　When night had spread its gloom.

When autumn came, in sadness,
　I wandered in the vale—
Alas! no song of gladness
　Was borne upon the gale;
But breezes chill were sweeping
　Through the branches of the trees—
They sound like fairies weeping
　A dirge for Hebe Lees!

Sweet forms in angel brightness
　Were moving 'neath the trees,
Their garments of pure whiteness
　Were waving in the breeze:
My heart was torn asunder,
　They bore the lovely maid,
And came and laid her under
　The elm-tree's gentle shade.

A funeral train attending
　Her body to the tomb,
And plaintive voices blending,
　Bewailed her early doom.
And now she sings in heaven,
　And wears a diadem,
The winds have power given
　To chant her requiem.

L

TO MAY.

The black thorn bloom falls from the spray,
  The daisies deck the hills,
And May, the lovely maiden, May,
  With joy each blossom fills:
Sweet May! the lark doth hail thee here,
  The linnet on the tree,
With thee the summer birds appear,
  The lambs call after thee.

Weary with toil I wander, May!
  Within thy peaceful bowers,
Thou cheer'st me with thy merry lay,
  And strew'st my path with flowers.
The meadows near their diadem
  Of cowslips! shall I say
That every floweret is a gem,
  To deck thy kirtle, May?

With the blossoms on thy brow, May!
  The primrose at thy feet,
And in thy hand the hawthorn spray,
  So fragrant and so sweet,
Thou bring'st the lilac to the bower,
  The lily to the grot,
And to the bank that bonnie flower,
  The sweet forget-me-not!

How beautiful thou art, fair May!
  In robes of gold and green!
How happy is thy roundelay,
  Thy face, May, how serene!
And on thy cheek the virgin blush,
  So beautiful to see,
And in the grove the sweet song-thrush
  Is carolling to thee!

A thousand birds their joy betray,
  To burst each bud is rife,
And when thou smil'st fair maiden, May!
  Earth teems with love and life.
So softly breathing, sweetest May!
  How balmy is the air!
I see thee tripping o'er the way,
  A vision bright and fair.

JENNY'S SNOWDROP.

This faded snowdrop I have cherished
   Through storm and sunshine many years,
And though its lovely tints are perished,
   It makes me think of Jenny's tears.

Fair Jenny was a lovely maiden,
   As blithe as any bird or bee,
We roamed the high-wood flower laden,
   My bonnie bright-eyed Jane and me.

But, ah! sweet Jenny crossed the billow,
   And she has perished there I fear;
For when asleep upon my pillow,
   Morpheus whispers in my ear:—

"Fair Jenny's lovely form lies sleeping,
   With wreath of coral on her brow,
And Syrens o'er her watch are keeping,
   In the rude halls of Neptune now."

So the fair young maiden perished,
   No tidings of her ever came,
For years this snowdrop I have cherished,
   And called it by sweet Jenny's name.

It bids me think of that fair morning,
   When it was plucked off by the maid,
The soft green tints its leaves adorning—
   Like all earth's offspring, it must fade.

THE TALKING OX.

"Now that Christmas day is coming,
   I tremble here the while,
For the money-making butcher
   Hath been across the stile.

"But ere the blue-coat gets me,
   And quits me with his knife,
I'll make my will and bequest,
   While I have got my life.

" The baron's for my master,
  The good rump for the priest,
And the man that reared and fed me,
  Shall have a jolly feast.

" To him I leave my bonny head,
  It will take some stewing,
The priest must tell him to be thankful
  With his Christmas brewing.

" The rest must go unto the State,
  But only just in time,
Here the butcher comes, exclaiming,
  ' Your ox, John, he is prime!'

" ' Ah! not only prime, but gentle,'
  Is faithful John's reply—
I am sorry that the noble beast,
  Should ever have to die.'

" And as I pass the faithful man,
  I see he sheds a tear,
And saith, ' I seem to love the beast,
  That I have fed this year.'

" Ah! now I find he is my friend,
  I long to make redress,
I should have left my feeder more,
  The greedy master less.

" O, is there no place to shelter
  From this blue-coat man?
Yes, the good priest's gate is open—
  Go in there I can.

" So I go into the garden
  Of the tender-hearted priest,
He strikes me with a stake, and saith—
  ' Go out you surly beast.'

" 'Tis now I think about my friend,
  And long to make redress,
I should have left my feeder more,
  The callous pastor less.

" But of the oxen I may pass,
  I'll say to every one —
If you should ever make your will,
  Remember faithful John."

TO VICTORY OR DEATH.

AN EPISTLE TO M. H.

Author of " Poetic Buds," " Wayside Blossoms," &c.

DEAR friend,—you ask what is my plan ?
To give unto my fellow man
Those tender sprays and leaflets frail,
When all the world doth at me rail.
'Tis now I stand nerved for the fray,
To make the stubborn foe give way,
To bend the sword, to split the lance,
And turn away the wrathful glance,
       To victory or death.

I am resolved, before my power
The mail-clad foe his crest shall lower,
I'll turn aside the poisoned dart,
Sent by envy at my heart.
The morning's blush afar I see,
Ere long the sun will shine on me,
And gladdened by his cheering ray,
I'll climb the rough and thorny way
       To victory or death.

And if at last my shield should fail,
And darts should shatter all my mail,
And lightning flash from pole to pole,
And bursting thunders fright my soul,
Methinks I'd die when rain drops fell,
And leave my little ones to tell,
He fell beneath the rainbow's arch,
When on his rough and thorny march
       To victory or death.

———

THIS WORLD IS NOT THE WILDERNESS THAT MAN WOULD MAKE IT BE.

COME leave the city and its din,
    And wander forth with me,
And pluck the wild rose from the hedge
    In virgin purity.

And list the lark uprising sing,
    And never more repine,
It bears the impress on its wing
    Of one who is divine.

What say the flowers of varied dress
　　That bloom upon the lea—
This world is not the wilderness
　　That man would make it be.

The lovely lily of the dell
　　That lives a life so pure,
The violet and pimpernell
　　So fragrant and demure.

The daisy as it looks above,　　　　　•
　　The king-cup's golden hue,
The rosebud with its voice of love
　　So eloquent and true,

The speedwell in its sky-blue dress
　　Are teachers all to me—
This world is not the wilderness
　　That man would make it be.

But let the deeds of man be told
　　Since first on earth he came,
In all his actions we behold
　　The stamp of Adam's name,

Then let us leave him in his rage,
　　And unto nature turn,
And gaze on that unblemished page
　　Where he who runs may learn.

What saith the linnet as it sings
　　Upon the hawthorn tree—
This world is not the wilderness
　　That man would make it be.

God's world is lovely every-where,
　　The mountains or the lea,
Yea, when the winter clothes the earth
　　With robes of purity.

Or when the summer o'er the land
　　Spreads verdure fresh and green,
The ocean too is truly grand
　　In tempest or serene.

And as I walk God's lovely earth
　　Some angel saith to me—
This world is not the wilderness
　　That man would make it be.

TO THE READER.

DEAR reader, hark! the cock is crowing,
   Yet the morning light is pale,
I hear the healthy breezes blowing,
   Over mountain, meadow, vale.

The anvil of the smith is ringing,
   Labour calls me to its mart,
And I awhile must cease my singing,
   And with you, dear reader, part.

And should you be a blushing Laura,
   Wander maid where I have been,
And rest you on the lap of Flora,
   In the fields of gold and green.

How often, when my path was dreary,
   I have rambled in the fields,
And when with toil my frame was weary,
   I felt the joy that nature yields.

And ah, its works need no rehearsal,
   They bespeak a master mind,
Nature's God is universal,
   To no narrow creed confined.

And if you be a toiling brother,
   Let not vice your soul delude,
When cares fall thick and fain would smother,
   Hie you to the solitude.

For there when woods and groves were ringing,
   I have felt a healing balm ;
With linnet, thrush, and blackbird singing,
   I have joined in nature's psalm.

To sing belongs not to the pheasant,
   Nor the peacock strutting past,
But oft upon the lowly peasant,
   The " mantle of the muse is cast."

Then, farewell, reader, sage, or student!
   Nature's path will e'er be trod ;
Nor frown upon me, statesman prudent !
   Nor thou—thou holy man of God.

www.ingramcontent.com/pod-product-compliance
Lightning Source LLC
Chambersburg PA
CBHW032349020726
47499CB00008B/2684